NEANDER

Also by Harald Johnson

Nonfiction
Mastering Digital Printing, Editions 1 & 2
Digital Printing Start-Up Guide

Fiction
The Manhattan Series (novella ebooks)
1609 (Book 1)
1612 (Book 2)
1625 (Book 3)
1640 (Book 4)

New York 1609: A Historical Novel
(Omnibus Edition)

NEANDER

A Time Travel Adventure

Harald Johnson

P
PHOOZL, LLC
Charlottesville, Virginia

Copyright © 2019 by Harald Johnson. All rights reserved.

Published by Phoozl, LLC, Charlottesville, Virginia
http://haraldjohnson.com

Cover and book design/formatting by Harald Johnson

This is a work of fiction. Apart from actual (real) people, events, and locations included in the narrative, all other characters, dialogue, events, and locations are the product of the author's imagination or are used fictitiously.

No part of this book may be reproduced, or stored in a retrieval system, or transmitted in any form or by any means, electronic, mechanical, photocopying, recording, or otherwise, without express written permission of the author or publisher.

ISBN: 9781710999105

Edition 1, Revision 0

For Lynn

*"Life can only be understood backwards;
but it must be lived forwards."*
— Søren Kierkegaard

"The past is never dead. It's not even past."
— William Faulkner

PART ONE

The Ring

1

I didn't like caves.

Fears of getting stuck in them had often swamped my dreams. To find myself now working in one—and fighting off the panic sweats—was certainly ironic. But that's where the best archeological evidence tended to be. I lived with it as best I could.

My hands shook as I rechecked the photo equipment and my to-do list again. Then I headed back out to the cave's entrance. Time to breathe. And call Carolyn.

I rested against the rim of Meredith's Cave, pulled out my phone, and took in the sight of the Mediterranean spread out in front of me. The sea was calming.

A late morning sun danced and sparkled on the surface of the water that surrounded Gibraltar. Gulls squawked and wheeled overhead hoping for a handout.

I spotted the whale-watching boat in the distance and pressed Carolyn's face icon on the phone. She picked up on the second ring.

"Hey, dad-to-be," she said.

"Is it great out there?" I asked, hoping—wishing—she wasn't too upset about my sending her off on another excursion by herself.

This was supposed to be a fun, together-trip to southern Spain. She was nearing the seven-month mark of her pregnancy, and this was her last opportunity to travel for a while.

"It's amazing. We've already seen two pilot whales and a pod of dolphins. And Africa's *right there*. I can almost touch it!"

Good. She sounded happy.

"How's it going in the cave?" she asked.

"Fine," I lied. "They've worked down another centimeter."

The reality was, the tension was thick. And that was apart from the claustrophobia.

My assignment was to document the excavation's progress for *Science Alive*, but my pushing to get it right with the lighting and the camera angles was annoying everyone. I knew that. But what were a few more minutes of attention to detail with a Neanderthal fossil that had been in the ground for tens of thousands of years?

I reached into my pants pocket and fingered the small, velvet ring box. I would propose to my beautifully pregnant Carolyn at dinner tonight. A thought that made me both nervous and excited.

I wanted this family so much.

"You're not being too anal with them, are you?" she asked.

"Who me?"

She was one of the few who understood my need for order, for perfection.

"Oh, there's another whale! Gotta go."

The phone beeped and the call was gone.

Till tonight, I mumbled to the gulls.

I started to put the phone away when it buzzed with another call. It was my editor in New York.

"Ron. What's up?" It was either very early or late for him.

"You busy?"

Stupid question. "Yes. What is it?"

There was a long pause before he said, "We have to cut you back."

I wasn't sure I heard right.

"What?"

"I said we need to cut you back."

"My time?"

"No. Your pay."

"My pay? I'm barely making ends meet."

"Look, you're on the high side of scale for a science publication, and the drop in online advertising and subs just can't support it. Sorry."

Prick. He wasn't sorry at all.

"So what's the good news?" I asked.

"We're broadening your scope," he said, not missing a beat. "Giving you culture, too. You'll be the science *and* culture reporter. Should be fun."

"Culture? For a science pub?"

"You know, like ancient civilizations. More humans, less animals."

"*Fewer* animals," I corrected.

"Whatever. Like what you're doing now on that Gibraltar dig. But focused more on what prehistoric people were really like. How they lived. What they ate. Where they pooped. That sort of thing. Our research shows strong interest in this."

I couldn't believe what I was hearing. Cutting my pay and giving me more work in the bargain.

"But my benefits are still there, right? Medical, 401k, life insurance. No change in that, right?"

"Right. No change. You're covered."

Well, that was something. With the baby coming the coverage was important. I needed this job. My new family needed this job.

I didn't know what else to say so I ended the call and just stared at the phone.

"Tom!" a volunteer shouted as he ran up behind me. "You gotta come quick. We need you." He was panting, eyes wild.

"What's so urgent?" I asked, following him back into the depths of the cave.

"You'll see," he said over his shoulder. "And you're

not going to believe it."

♦ ♦

The whole team was crowded around the find. Brushes and trowels and dental picks were put aside. Some of the volunteers balanced on wood planks while others stood on scaffolding beams.

All were focused on one thing: the point where dig director Victoria Busher's spotlight shone with a bluish light on the fossil's hand.

"What is it?" I asked, stepping carefully on the structure built up around the skeletal remains.

I was trying to get close, while at the same time double-checking that no one had moved my flash stands. I had pre-positioned them in the cramped space so whenever I took a shot the flashes fired simultaneously and gave me the kind of fully-lit images I liked.

Without shifting her light, Victoria twisted her head back to me and said matter-of-factly, "Get your camera."

I did.

Crouching, I concentrated on the small object the hominid skeleton—nicknamed Meredith for the cave—appeared to be showing off on the little finger of its left hand.

"It's a ring!" I said as I moved in closer, lighting up the cave with each press of the camera shutter.

I sat back on my heels to think for a moment.

"Did Neanderthals wear rings?"

Victoria looked puzzled. Not answering, she leaned in holding a special magnifying glass with tiny LED lights spaced around its edge.

"Well I'll be damned," she said after a few seconds. "It's a gold finger ring with a real diamond." She let out a short whistle as murmurs filled the cave.

"Rings can last for thousands of years?" I asked.

"Depends," she said while she moved closer and repositioned the magnifier. "Setting aside the fact that metallurgy and gem cutting wouldn't be invented for another 35,000 years or so, if the ring is 18 karat gold with a real diamond, then yes.

"This diamond is still perfect, but the gold has tarnished slightly. Probably from one of the alloy metals. If it were 24 karats there'd be no tarnish at all. But 24-karat gold is too soft for jewelry."

I immediately felt dizzy and had to use a hand to prop myself and then take in several deep breaths. That was the exact question I had discussed with the saleswoman in the Gibraltar jewelry story last week before buying the ring in my pants pocket. I had settled on an 18-karat gold band even though 14 karats was much less expensive. I was going all out for Carolyn.

But it wasn't the similarity of components that left me slack-jawed. After I took another close-up look at the ring, it was all I could do to keep from hyperventilating.

It *was* Carolyn's ring.

2

While the team went to work picking, troweling, and brushing to expose more of the skeletal hand from the calcified sediments and sand that encased it—it had separated from the arm at the wrist—I retreated to give them room to work, first checking my flash positions again.

I found an isolated area close to the cave opening and pulled out the ring box from my trousers.

Confirming that no one was nearby, I quickly opened the box and stared at the ring, still lying on its velvet bed.

It was exactly the same ring!

How was this possible?

Of course, chances were good there would be more than one copy of the ring being sold here and there.

But that didn't explain how a modern ring ended up on the fossil finger of a Neanderthal buried at the back end of a Pleistocene-era cave.

Was this some kind of trick?

I heard footsteps and pushed the ring back into my pants before turning.

It was Victoria. Tall, thin, and agitated. A strained smile. Troubled green eyes. Worried about her career, no doubt.

"Listen," she said in that distinctively deep voice of hers. "We've had our history, but we need to get our heads together on this."

I nodded without speaking.

"Got to keep a lid on this ring thing," she continued. "I know you like to get the images out as quickly as possible, especially if you're preparing a story. But this has to stay in-house for the moment. It's just too bizarre."

Bizarre would be a mild description of the situation if she knew about the ring in my pocket.

I studied her attractive face, framed by red hair and sprinkled with fine sand. And noticed a trickle of sweat working its way down her forehead. The cave was cool, which meant she was nervous.

"You think it's a prank?" I asked. "Another Piltdown Man?"

That hoax about finding the missing link between ape and man had fooled a lot of people. Even experts who should have known better.

"God, I hope not," she said, "but I don't see any rational explanation for this. I mean, worked gold? Diamond cutting? It's not possible."

Her expression suddenly changed, and she put a hand on my arm. I knew that touch and sensed her wanting to revive something between us, so I stepped back, letting her hand fall. She was looking for a familiar closeness I could no longer allow.

Dr. Victoria Busher and I had a background.

Former lovers as undergrads at the University of Texas, she'd become a star of paleoanthropology while I had dropped out to work in science journalism. We'd rekindled the flame whenever we ended up at conferences or on digs like this one.

But once I met Carolyn, I cut it off cold with Victoria. Something it took her ego a long time to accept.

She glowered for a moment then lifted her head, letting the moment pass.

"So, how's the job?" she asked, thankfully changing the subject.

"Pretty much crap," I said honestly. "They keep cutting back and merging positions."

"Doing more with less, right?"

"Yep. I thought I was a science journalist, and now they want me to handle culture, too. Soon, I'll be reporting on celebrity gossip." I made a show of shuddering.

"And what does Carolyn say about this?"

"She's supportive but—"

A loud *BOOM!* blasted. An explosion from

somewhere outside the cave that vibrated the air inside it.

We both looked at each other and instinctively started sprinting to the entrance.

◆ ◆

I shaded my eyes and stared in disbelief. Directly out from the cave, about a half-mile offshore, the whale-watching boat burned and smoked.

Panic mixed with nausea as I frantically tried to dial Carolyn's cell phone. I kept missing the icon but finally got it. It rang until her voicemail came on.

"Hi, you've reached Carolyn. Please leave—"

"Carolyn!" I shouted. "Pick up, pick up." *Oh God, please pick up.*

"Tom, are you sure—" Victoria started. "Maybe—"

"It's her boat!" I screamed at her.

She flinched and took a step back.

"Sorry," I said before returning to the horrible sight. A large plume of black smoke rose from the boat that now sat lower in the water.

I automatically started tapping my chest with my right hand in a steady rhythm. This was one of my calming routines when I found myself under high stress. My mind was doing somersaults and my knees started to shake.

"I— I've got to *do* something. I've got to get out there."

"But—"

Not thinking, just reacting, I started running along the roped walkway that led to the cave entrance.

"To do what?" I heard Victoria's voice behind me as I picked up speed down the slope and vaulted over a low retaining wall.

"Whatever I can," I shouted into the wind that now brought the first whiffs of smoke.

♦ ♦

I hadn't thought through the alternatives. I'd just scrambled over the rocks, stripped down to my underpants, and started swimming.

Should I have gone back up to the road and worked my way around to the boat dock to get more information? Maybe. But I'd committed myself.

I was a good swimmer and a half-mile was no problem. Especially in water that was warmer than my usual at home in Los Angeles in October.

The adrenaline was pumping while I swam straight out toward the ominous threads of smoke. What I would do when I got there, I had no idea. But I had to do something. I was taking the only action I was sure of.

Halfway there, a small boat suddenly appeared on my breathing side and I stopped.

"Hey man, what you doing?" asked the young Spaniard steering the boat. He had a mop of black hair, thick eyebrows, and intense blue eyes.

I pointed ahead. "The boat," I said between breaths. "Got to get there."

I saw him glance up then back to me with a doubtful look.

"Dios mío. The burning boat?"

"Yeah. And you're wasting my time."

He shook his head and blew out a sound through his lips.

"You crazy, man. But come on. Get in. I take you *rápidamente.*"

I quickly studied him and his dented aluminum skiff then looked ahead toward the sinking boat and made an instant decision. He could help me in more ways than one.

I held up a hand and he grabbed it.

"Let's go, amigo."

3

It was chaos around the sinking boat. Burned survivors—many screaming—were trying to reach two police vessels now on the scene.

Some of the officers hauled the swimmers in while others ineffectively aimed small, handheld fire extinguishers at the flaring wreckage.

The boat itself was hard to recognize. Only pieces of hull and cabin were still visible above the waterline. Everything in flames hissed and spat as it sank.

A thick trail of dark smoke now blocked out the afternoon sun. The smell was a mix of burning fiberglass and something living. Human flesh?

Several other private craft had also arrived and everyone was yelling out advice to everyone else, including the Royal Gibraltar Police.

"Head over to the police boats," I shouted to my new accomplice, Santiago, who had tossed me a thin windbreaker to put on.

He twisted the throttle of the outboard motor and we jolted away.

As we closed in on the first boat I shouted her name. "Carolyn! Carolyn!"

Hearing no reply, we moved to the next boat and I called her name again. And again, nothing.

I was frantic. It was time to put my freediving experience to use.

"Stay here," I instructed Santiago. Then I pulled off the windbreaker, grabbed a quick breath, and dove into the water.

I tasted oil and cleared my ears as I went down, kicking and pulling my way toward what looked like the wrecked boat. I didn't have goggles or a mask so my vision was blurry, but I could feel the heat in the water. I aimed for the source of it.

I reached the main part of the burned-out hull about 35 feet down. It was sitting on a sandy bottom, charred and ruined. And wedged up against an enormous mound of stones that looked like one of those cairns meant as memorials or landmarks. But why so far underwater?

I was out of air so I headed back for the surface.

"It's there," I gasped while Santiago motored over. I pointed straight down. "Stay here. I'll try again."

He nodded and cut his engine to idle.

I dove once more and moved through the boat's hulk more methodically, touching everything I could. The light was dim but it was enough to see basic shapes. I only stopped when I felt something soft. Some were trapped and drowned bodies, and I quickly scanned their faces. No Carolyn. I continued until I needed air again.

I came up, brushing against the side of one of the police boats.

"Get out of the water!" came the British-accented command from the bullhorn. The man holding it wore a dark blue uniform and he was angry. "This is a crime scene. Not a place for you."

He turned to Santiago and barked something in the local Llanito idiom that was too quick for me to understand.

Santiago lowered his hand over the side to me but I slapped it away.

"I have to find my fiancée!" I yelled at the man with the bullhorn.

"No," he snarled back, leaning down. "That's our job." He tilted his head and squinted. "Unless..."

He turned to two other men and ordered, "Grab him."

Before I knew it, I was in the police boat wrapped in a blanket, both hands cuffed together. Still in my underpants.

Santiago stood in his skiff by his engine with a shocked look on his face.

"Meet me back in town," I shouted to him. "But go find my clothes on the shore by the caves first." I gestured in the direction.

He nodded and gave me a tentative wave.

I waved back with my manacled hands and felt the police boat lurch and start moving away from the awful scene while more boats approached. A few smoldering pieces from the wreck still bobbed on the water as the sun finally touched the western horizon.

I stood against the rail and pulled the blanket tighter around me against the stiff wind. The panic had subsided but the idea of losing Carolyn—and the baby—was unbearable.

I focused on my breath and started tapping my chest.

Stay calm, I repeated again and again.

It's not over yet.

◆ ◆

"You can go," the same officer said, uncuffing me. We were in a small room at the police station. A single fluorescent light buzzed overhead. The smell of sweat permeated the room.

I stared at his shiny bald head and the emblem stitched on his shoulder. *RGP Marine Section.*

"So what happened to the boat?" I asked, still wrapped in the blanket.

"Under investigation."

"Was it an accident or terrorism?"

He studied me with bagged eyes. "No comment. But when we see someone lingering near an explosion like that, it makes us wonder."

I could see his point.

"But we're quite sure it wasn't you. You have an alibi."

"Good to know, but my pregnant fiancée—Carolyn—was on the boat and I need to find her." The desperation washed over me again.

"Just stay out of the water and away from that wreck," he said sternly.

He handed me a plastic bag. "Your clothes, from the boatman. He's outside. And the mortuary's downstairs if you want to check there." His voice revealed a hint of emotion.

He opened the room's door and stood aside, pointing. "You can change down the hall."

As I passed, he put a hand on my arm. "I'm terribly sorry for your loss."

After changing into my clothes and thankfully finding the ring still in my pants, I emerged into a noisy room crowded with people.

Many were sobbing. Others were crowded at a high counter both asking and demanding in English, Spanish, and Llanito about their loved ones.

Some were polite but others weren't, shouting at the frazzled officers who were trying to explain that they were doing the best they could to locate and account for everyone in the explosion.

I spotted Santiago standing next to Victoria near a

window in the corner. It was dark outside.

I nodded to Victoria and shook Santiago's hand and thanked him for his help and for returning my clothes.

"Pues, es la que tú me haces, amigo."

I stared. I was good with languages but this was beyond me.

"It means: it's you that makes me this way." He grinned. "I like people with guts. Even British."

"I'm not British, I'm American. Californian."

"Even better, amigo. A risk-taker." He winked.

I pulled him close and spoke into his ear. "You available for more risks? To help more?" He seemed like a good local partner for whatever was needed.

"You know it, boss," he said, smiling.

"What are you two whispering about?" Victoria asked in her low-pitched voice.

I turned to her. "Nothing. He's the one who helped me in the water."

"I know," she said. "He filled me in. Your swimming out there was stupid, but I'm glad it worked out."

"Worked out?" I snapped. "I still haven't found Carolyn, have I? She could be . . ."

I took a deep breath. The impact of not knowing what had happened to Carolyn or where she was hit me hard again.

"I'm sorry." Victoria reached out a hand to me. "I wasn't thinking. What do you want to do?"

I took her hand and squeezed.

"Let's go find the morgue."

4

I put down the empty coffee cup and opened the local paper.

The *Gibraltar Chronicle* was filled with stories about the explosion, but what made me fold the paper in half and bring it close was the list. It was divided into two sections with bold subheads: "The Dead" and "Missing & Presumed Dead."

I moved my finger down until it stopped on Carolyn's name in the second part. She hadn't been in the morgue.

The restaurant was attached to the hotel on Cathedral Square near the museum that was involved with the dig. It was where many of the site workers ate. They had the traditional, full English breakfast, and I had taken a table tucked into a small side room.

Morning light never made it back this far, which was fine with me.

I wanted to be alone with my black thoughts. The ever-more-apparent death of Carolyn was a major shock, but just as strong was the feeling of outrage about the violent act itself.

The paper's cover story included an interview with a high-ranking official in the RGP.

"What kind of people would do this?"

"Terrorists. They care for nothing but themselves and their power. They want to destroy everything else."

"But why?"

"It's the way they are. The way we are. We're humans. Some good, some bad. I've seen both kinds."

No one had yet claimed credit but it would surely come. The scum who carried out these acts were never shy about their involvement after the fact.

And the cruel irony with Carolyn was not lost on me. She worked for an international aid group that helped victims of terrorism, and here she was listed in black and white as one of its victims.

Waves of utter sadness mixed with a familiar sensation of building panic as I thought about where Carolyn could be. Was she floating on the water somewhere? Or was she still down in that burned-out hulk on the seabed? Had the rescue divers missed her as I had?

Knowing that she believed strongly in the idea of a proper burial with the body present at the funeral, the thought of her being unaccounted for was unacceptable. Something had to be done. And I was prepared to do it.

I closed my eyes and focused on my breathing, letting it gradually slow itself and bring me back to something approaching an unagitated condition.

I heard a throat clear from the doorway. I opened my eyes to Victoria.

"Come in," I said, putting down the paper and nodding to the chair opposite me.

Victoria sat and glanced at the newspaper.

"I saw it. It's awful."

I nodded and pushed my barely touched breakfast across the table to her.

She shook her head *no*.

"Listen," she said, staring at me, clearly trying to judge my emotional state, "you don't need to come to the site today. You've got a lot—"

"No, I need to do some work. I want the diversion."

That was partially true. I wanted to let the day pass in some form of normal. But I also had to delay the next part of my plan.

I waited for her to leave before picking up my phone and dialing Santiago's number. He answered and I said quickly, "You ready for tonight?"

◆ ◆

With twilight descending on this tiny British overseas

territory attached to Spain like an appendix, I started to walk the few short blocks to the main dock and tried to shut out the sorrow and despair I was feeling about Carolyn. And the baby. He was—would be—a boy, and we had already named him. Devin.

The grief tore at me. So I diverted my attention to what I was seeing around me on my walk through Gibraltar.

It was almost mid-October and the wind was now from the west—the *Pointiente* they called it. It brought in cooler sea currents from the Atlantic, but it was nothing I wasn't used to in the cold Pacific off the coast of West Los Angeles.

I still marveled at the fact that I had traded one Mediterranean climate for another, although Gibraltar was slightly more humid overall. Which is why I was wearing only shorts and a T-shirt.

I'd put in a half-hearted day at the dig site, thinking mostly about Carolyn and my preparations. Victoria noticed my lack of enthusiasm and finally told me to quit and go back to the hotel. But instead of resting, I spent the next few hours planning and gathering up the needed equipment.

The smell of spilled beer and frying grease assaulted me as I passed one pub after another full of tourists and Thank-God-it's-Friday British expats spilling into the street.

I was pushing my way through the crowd outside a noisy bar when a door splintered and two men crashed through. People formed a circle and shouted encouragement as the brawling men, both clearly drunk, fought each other.

The crowd, holding their beers and fish-and-chips baskets aloft, then closed in on the men and started to chant: "*kill him, kill him!*"

I stepped away but couldn't take my eyes off the two men—both spent but still punching and kicking—and the bloodthirsty looks on the faces of the onlookers. Everyone seemed to have entered a force field of violence and viciousness.

What was in their minds to do this, and how much different was it from the mental state of the boat bombers?

Disgusted, I turned my back on the ugly scene and headed down the street, the sound of shouting and chanting slowly fading away as I turned a corner and saw the water ahead of me.

I spotted Santiago's skiff tied up next to the dock in the harbor. It was easily the smallest and least-flashy boat in the marina, and that brought me relief. You couldn't get more under the radar than this.

"*Hola, Señor California,*" Santiago said as he reached out to help me with the gear. "What do you have there?"

I handed him two large mesh bags and stepped onto the boat while gripping my fins.

"Just some of my freediving gear: wetsuit, low-volume mask, snorkel, headlamp, and some other things." I raised the long fins. "And these babies."

He took the fins from me and held them out for inspection.

"Wow, where do you dive to, China?"

I explained that the longer fins were more efficient and used less energy.

"No tanks? No scuba?" he asked, bewildered.

"No. I'm good at this. Tanks can get in the way in tight spaces."

"If you say so, boss." He waved his arm over the length of his boat. "I'm only captain of your luxury yacht, and, how you say, *a su servicio.*"

"At my service, and I appreciate that."

I put a hand to his shoulder.

"Look, I know this is risky for you. There are rules and laws, and you have to deal with the marine police."

"Screw the police," he said, grinning. "They are British and it's our water, not theirs. *¡Gibraltar español!*"

I grinned back and nodded. Then I felt for the ring that now hung from an impromptu shoelace necklace under my shirt.

"*Ándale, pues!*" I said using my best Mexican-Spanish phrase for getting a move on.

Santiago laughed and started up the engine.

5

We didn't talk while Santiago motored out of the harbor and turned south.

He kept the engine on low throttle so we barely made any noise while skimming the water. He had insisted on keeping his running lights on here—"they see no lights and come to us in seconds"—but we were now officially on a stealth mission to locate Carolyn.

I checked my watch: 8:30 p.m. It was nautical twilight and the sky still held a trace of its luminance, but we'd soon be running in full darkness. A cloud cover had turned off the stars, and the moon was new so we'd have no light from her either.

The winds had eased off as they always did at the end of the day, and after we rounded Europa Point with Trinity House Lighthouse on our port side and

Morocco's coast on our starboard, Santiago opened the throttle and the boat raced forward. The dark emptiness of the whole Mediterranean lay ahead. Only the sprinkle of lights from both shorelines framed the blackness in front of us.

I asked, "You'll be able to find the place again?"

"Of course," he said, looking down at the GPS monitor's glowing screen. "This and the lights of Ceuta and Gibraltar are my good friends. I know the waters."

"I'm sure you do. And no police or salvage boats to worry about?"

He chuckled. "No, boss. They eat and drink. No one works too hard here."

I was about to come back with something clever when my cell phone rang. It was Victoria.

"Hey, I knocked on your door and thought I'd invite you down for a drink. I'm worried about you. You okay? And what's that noise? Are you outside?"

I cradled the phone with both hands trying to shut out the sound of the whining engine.

"Yeah, I'm fine. Thanks. Just taking a walk. Can't really talk right now. Catch up tomorrow?"

"Sure. Whatever you need."

We hung up.

I felt bad about deceiving her, but my focus was on Carolyn.

Was I kidding myself in thinking I might actually find her? Even with the far-fetched idea that she was still alive? Maybe washed up on a beach somewhere?

The anguish of not knowing her fate was oppressive. That sound of the boat explosion boomed repeatedly in my head. I had to take this final step to make sure.

"Family?" Santiago asked over the motor noise.

"No, the one you met at the police station. My supervisor here. Victoria."

"Ah, her. Low voice. Very serious. Not crazy like you."

"Crazy?"

He laughed softly. "I mean to make the risks. Do what it takes."

I could see the dark shape of his body turned to me.

"Oh, she also does what it takes all right. Trust me."

We motored on in silence. Then the phone chirped. It was a text, not a call. Now what?

It was from my editor, Ron. I opened it up.

Have heard. Really sorry. But can we get something from you? Pix? Draft text? Anything? Deadline coming.

Jesus. Just what I needed. I flipped the phone over, screen down.

Santiago suddenly turned off the running lights and throttled back.

I said, "We're getting close?"

"*Sí.*"

We stopped.

"Over the cairn? The rock pile?"

"*Sí. Mojón.*"

"Why is it down there?"

"No one knows. But the fish, they like it. So it means

I like it."

He laughed and I saw his white teeth shine in the light of the GPS screen.

I took my time putting on the gear. Although it was a warm night, and with my T-shirt off, I still donned my long-sleeved wetsuit top. The marine depths were good at chilling the body to its core. And a high core temperature was the only weapon I had against hypothermia, which would quickly end the search.

After I had the wetsuit over my shorts, I pulled on the fins. I spat into the mask and rinsed it overboard before positioning and adjusting it on my face. I checked the angle of the snorkel against my left temple then slipped on the headlamp.

Finally, I reached under my wetsuit and rubbed the diamond ring on its rawhide necklace. For luck.

"*Estoy listo*," I said, sitting on the edge of the boat's hull. Ready.

"Then *buena suerte* my friend. I wait for you."

I gave him a thumbs-up before I took a final breath and fell backward into the cold, dark water.

◆ ◆

It was coal-black heading down until I turned on my headlamp. Suddenly the sea came alive. Swarms of tiny fish darted away through a water column that was full of plankton and other aquatic microorganisms.

Kicking easily and clearing my ears again, I spotted

the cairn and the wreck below me and made a beeline for them.

The search-and-rescue divers would have recovered all the bodies from the wreck by now. But even though the chance of finding Carolyn was remote, I still had to try. And maybe I could find *something* connected to her: keys, binoculars, a jacket. Anything.

As my light raked the edge of the pyramid of stone I saw something I had missed before. Moving away to get a wider view, I recognized a clear pattern spiraling around the cairn from top to bottom.

This was not a random pile of rocks. Someone had gone to a lot of trouble to make an artistic design. It reminded me of the whorling shell of a nautilus.

Immobilized by the beauty of it, I just hung in the water and stared at the stones before I remembered my purpose.

I put my head down and did a couple of quick kicks that brought me to the wreck. I didn't have much air left so I could only start on my close-up search inside the charred hull.

Using a practiced visual trick I'd taught myself over the years, I squinted my eyes and slowly moved my head from side to side, hoping to catch something in my peripheral vision.

There were bits and pieces of the boat's structure scattered about, and also signs of life on the deck in the last moments: a coffee mug, a hat, a camera. But my lungs were seizing so I headed for the surface.

I grabbed the skiff's rail and took in gulps of air.

"I'm finding things," I said to Santiago between breaths. "Not *her* things yet, but I have a feeling there's something of Carolyn's down there. One more dive."

Santiago's head shot up. *"Mierda.* They spot us."

I turned and immediately saw the flashing blue light. And it was coming our way fast.

"Make up a story," I said, taking in two deep, controlled breaths. "I'll be under for a minute or more."

I bent at the waist, raised one leg, and kicked my way back down.

Once I reached the wreck I went to the last-explored spot and restarted my search.

Gently touching and moving away whatever would move, I glimpsed a familiar item. One kick and I was on it.

It was an iPhone. *Her* iPhone. She had laughed when she showed me the leopard-fur case she'd bought for it. "Ready to pounce and drag you up a tree for later eating," was her joke.

I quickly scanned the immediate area near the phone for other objects but found nothing connected to her.

Tucking the phone under the bottom of my wetsuit, I turned off my headlamp and looked up. The flashing blue light was almost above me. So much for my secret mission.

I closed my eyes, instinctively pressed on the ring through the neoprene, and started up with a slow kick, running through possible excuses and explanations.

Maybe I'd had a dream. Maybe her departed soul had reached out to me. Maybe I could plead insanity.

As the thoughts bounced around inside my head, I started to sense something change. A shift in both pressure and temperature. There was a rippling in the water, like a large animal had just moved past. And a low-frequency groaning sound—I didn't know if I was hearing or feeling it—that made my body shiver.

My eyes popped open. I was close to the surface now and looked straight up.

And there was nothing there.

6

I came up starving for air and immediately began to suck it in. I'd been under longer than expected and my body was heaving from the high level of carbon dioxide.

But things were off. Way off.

There was no skiff, no police boat. And it was already getting light.

I lifted my mask and there was the Rock of Gibraltar in the distance. Still towering. But different.

I squinted. *Huh?* The caves were not at sea level. They were higher up the Rock. *How could . . .*

I slowly spun around, not believing what I was seeing. I wasn't treading water offshore in the area of the Mediterranean called the Alboran Sea. I was in water, all right, but it was more like a small lake, in the middle of a vast, sloping plain that angled down from the Rock. I saw grasses, marsh-like plants, bushes, and a few stunted trees. And lots of sand.

What the . . .

Then I froze. There was the cairn. Looming *over* me. Every stone dry as a bone.

It was light now and I spotted the sea's shoreline, finally, but it was far to the east and the south, at least a mile or so away. The snow-capped Rif Mountains of Morocco were there but that coast's shoreline was also closer. The Strait of Gibraltar had become impossibly narrow.

I felt my head tightening, and I knew the panic and vertigo were coming. I started counting and pressing my thumbs to each finger. *One, two, three . . .*

I was anxious and starting to get dizzy. But who wouldn't be?

I mean, where was I?

I had to get out of the water and onto dry land. If only to lie down and compose myself. I needed normal.

Tasting water that was more fresh than salty, I swam to the edge of the lake nearest the cairn and walked out of the water on my hands until I could kneel on dry sand. I didn't want to take a chance of standing and getting dizzier.

I pulled off my fins and crawled up to the base of the cairn and sat against it, leaning my back on one of the larger stones, looking toward the Rock. I noticed that the air was much cooler than I remembered from yesterday. Or was it yesterday?

I saw no boats, buildings, people, or for that matter, anything that looked like a busy shipping channel and a developed shoreline. And there was no noise except for the wind and the far-off calling of seagulls.

I stayed like this for a long time—hours—going through my relaxation techniques one by one: slowly breathing in and out, tapping, pressing. Anything familiar.

The vertigo gradually retreated and I felt better physically, but mentally I was a mess. Was I dreaming? Imagining? Or—*oh no*—time-traveling?

That final thought stayed in the front of my brain, niggling at me. Had I crossed some kind of time threshold? Was I in the same place but not in 2019? In the future? In the past? Was I hallucinating all this? Was I losing my mind?

Finally, with hunger gnawing in my gut, I watched the sky begin to darken. I had lost a day. Maybe more. What was my next move? What was the plan? I needed one badly. Something to latch onto. Items and tasks to order. A list to check. I closed my eyes and started to build one in my head.

I was thinking about food when I heard a high-pitched growl and snapped to attention, eyes wide open.

In the dimming light, I saw several dark forms moving. They looked like large dogs. And they were circling me.

As my dark vision improved and the animals started

barking and moving closer, my panic level spiked. I looked around for a weapon but saw nothing.

I was inching myself to my feet when one of the animals charged. At that same moment, something or someone grabbed my wetsuit top and yanked me up against the cairn. But not before I felt teeth clamp down hard on my lower leg.

"Aowww!" I shouted while intense pain surged through me.

I looked down to see the beast's head shaking and trying to drag me back. It seemed more like a hyena than a dog. It had spots on its back.

I braced both hands against the cairn to stop my downward movement.

Then suddenly I was bumping against every stone and being roughly pulled up and out of reach of the beasts, now snarling and leaping, trying to seize my legs in their white-fanged mouths.

I tried to look up to see who or what was pulling me, but my head started spinning and all the color drained from my eyes.

◆ ◆

When I came to, I was lying on hard stone and looking up at the bluest sky I'd ever seen. I guessed it to be mid-morning, and I was still confused.

Where was I? When was I?

I rolled onto my stomach and looked down over the

edge of the cairn. Thankfully, the hyenas or dogs, or whatever they were, were gone.

Sensing I was not alone, I sat up then jerked back. There was a man, also sitting, no more than 10 feet from me. The one who must have saved me.

We both stared at each other across the small, flat area that formed the top of the pyramidal cairn. He was motionless. Studying me. And now I studied him.

He looked like something out of a movie about savages or cavemen. Random images from *Quest for Fire* flooded my mind.

He appeared to be younger than me, but it was hard to tell. He had long and unkempt hair with a scraggly beard and the makings of a mustache. He wore a loincloth of some type, and he had an animal skin draped over his powerful shoulders. Otherwise, he was basically naked.

And no shoes. I didn't have any either, but I had an excuse.

The man had a broad face and a big nose. He had a worn-out feeling about him, but his vivid azure eyes were alive with light and curiosity. He was an odd-looking fellow.

And he was smiling. Clearly not going to kill me. But the smile turned down when he looked at my leg.

He gestured with a bloody hand and said something I couldn't understand, but it sounded like a question. The voice was quiet, and the words tumbled out in a way that reminded me of birdsong. There was an up-and-down change in pitch and tone that sounded like warbling.

I'd forgotten about the leg wound in the surprise of seeing this strange man, but a wave of stabbing pain now brought my attention back to it.

The lower part of my right leg was a bloody mess. The flesh was torn, and I could see part of my tibia bone showing through. But I also saw bloody fingerprints on both sides of the wound. Evidence that someone had worked on it, applying pressure to stanch the bleeding. That explained the man's red hands.

Nothing felt broken but this was a serious injury, and something had to be done about it. Much of the blood had coagulated but some still oozed out.

The man suddenly stood up and nodded to my leg. He spoke more unintelligible words and pointed off the edge of the cairn.

He lifted both arms and pushed his hands toward me and downward. He repeated the motion.

Then he turned and disappeared over the side.

I was alone again.

My sense was that he was going to find or get something to help with the wound, and that I should stay put. But I wasn't sure.

The only sure thing was that I was on my own and injured. And confused about what the hell was going on.

But one thing was crystal clear. If I didn't get some help soon, I was going to die on top of this pile of rocks.

7

I lay on my back trying to soak up whatever warmth I could. Even with the sun high in the sky and blindingly bright, my exposed legs and head were cold. A constant wind whipped around the top of the cairn.

Luckily, I still had on my wetsuit top, and the black neoprene soaked in the sun and radiated warmth to my arms and torso.

In the panic of last night's attack, I'd lost the mask, snorkel, fins, and headlamp at the base of the cairn. Same for Carolyn's iPhone. Something told me that I wouldn't be needing them now.

Soon after the warbling man—I decided to call him Wren, for the songbird—had left, I did a little more observation and thinking. It helped take my mind off the painful throbbing of my leg.

This was definitely the same cairn I had been diving around. The spiral design was identical, and I could recognize specific stones near the bottom that I'd seen during my dives.

And the mystery of why it was out of the water was dawning on me.

This was an observation post of some kind. A high point to stand on and to see what was around. It reminded me of a hunter's tree blind. But without the tree.

And it wasn't the only one. Scanning carefully on all sides, I could spot more of the towers in a ragged, roughly east-west configuration. A line of elevated positions on a sloping plain that arced around this southern tip of what I knew was Gibraltar.

Of course! I realized, almost slapping my forehead with melodrama. During the time of the last Ice Ages, the world's sea level had dropped something like 100 meters because of all the water trapped in the ice sheets. So what had been submerged in 2019 was now exposed in . . . When? Thousands of years ago? Tens of thousands? Hundreds of thousands?

I mentally sifted through all the research I'd done prior to the dig. Victoria had sent me a folder of it, but I had gone much deeper, reading books and going online to locate obscure research papers in archeology and paleoanthropology.

Trying to process all this, I was rolling through my mental timeline of human ancestors when I heard

Wren climbing up the cairn. He soon rejoined me at the top, breathing hard. And bringing a sour odor with him. I wasn't sure if it was the animal skin or just his body.

I ignored the smell as he settled next to me and opened up a small sack that was bunched and tied at the top with a vine. Inside was a paste the color of dark mud and with the scent of pine sap. He dipped two thick fingers into it.

I knew immediately what it was: a poultice. Something to spread over a wound to help it heal. And optimistically to fight the risk of infection from an animal bite. At least that's what I hoped it was. And I had no way to ask for details.

Gritting my teeth against the pain from him spreading the poultice on the wound, I stole another glance at the short, stocky man.

His face was wide and it projected forward. He had a receding chin and his forehead sloped back giving his head a kind of aerodynamic shape. His exaggerated brow ridges shaded large, deep-set eyes that framed a broad nose. He reminded me of those scientific reconstructions of archaic humans.

Then it hit me. *Are you a Neanderthal?*

◆ ◆

We were on the move with me on his back, my arms clasped around his neck while his were folded under my legs. Piggyback style.

My head was on top of his, and his wild hair—a reddish-brown—tickled my face as he made progress avoiding obstacles and covering the sandy ground. We were heading toward the Rock.

I had hoped to get back into the lake and reverse the steps I'd taken to arrive in this puzzling place, but the leg wound was serious. I couldn't risk it. Whatever was happening to me, I needed to see this through. At least for a while longer.

The man was muscular and strong. He had to be to carry all 180 pounds of me on his back. But he also took frequent breaks. On the last one, he stopped and lowered me onto a large rock. Then he squatted in front and inspected my leg wound.

Blood seeped through the mud poultice. The pain had transitioned from searing to just aching, but I knew that bleeding to death was still a possibility for me. A growing wooziness told me that.

He was concerned too, and he spoke in that odd singsong way again. Not only did I not understand his words, but I'd never heard a voice like that before.

I had read conflicting studies about the language and speech capabilities of ancient hominid species. Some scientists hypothesized that speech was not possible for our human ancestors and "cousins" because of their different cranial and neck anatomies. Others said nonsense to that. Neanderthals and other archaic humans were physically capable of speech even if they hadn't developed the complex grammar and vocabulary that "modern humans" had conquered.

Scientists were constantly battling over these kinds of arguments, but how was that going to help me in my struggle to understand what was happening here?

Had I truly been transported to Paleolithic times? It was a surreal thought but the evidence was hard to ignore. The change in landscape matched what I knew, and the man carrying me matched the hominid recreations I'd studied in books and on museum visits.

Neanderthals—if that was what Wren was—had existed for hundreds of thousands of years, and I had apparently been dropped into their world.

It was all too much to contend with in my weakened state. My panic attacks and the need for control would have to wait. I had to focus on the present—the here and the now.

I lifted my head to find the sun. It was lower in the sky. He also looked up, grunted, then stood.

Wren turned around so I could climb onto his back again. He latched his muscular arms around my legs, and we started off once more like a two-person relay team at a child's picnic game.

I had no idea why he was helping me or where we were going. But we needed to get there soon if I was going to make it.

8

The smell of smoke roused me. I must have fainted on Wren's back.

We were climbing up a rocky slope to the entrance of a large cave. I blinked several times. It was Meredith's Cave!

A rough arch formed the mouth in the vertical cliff, and the rocks under our feet changed to sand as we approached the opening. This was the very place where I'd stood with Victoria, looking out on the Mediterranean, horrified by the sight of Carolyn's burning boat.

Bewilderment changed to amazement after we entered the cave. Lining both sides of the narrowing space were people. People who looked like Wren. Different ages of both sexes. About a dozen. And they stood silently watching as we passed by, moving deeper into the interior, the temperature rising as we did.

Wren said something and all of them grouped in behind us, following as we made our way farther into the cave.

We came to a stop and I was lowered gently to the ground. My injured leg had gone numb so I focused my attention on the immediate surroundings, trying to take it all in.

I felt cave anxieties forming but I pushed them down. No time for that now.

We were deep inside the cave and close to a large, snapping fire that blazed in the middle of a ring of stones. This provided most of the light and must have been the reason for the temperature change.

A stew of smells assaulted my nose: smoke and sweat and a moldy, musty stuffiness.

I tilted my head and watched the fire's smoke rise up to a high, vaulted ceiling—at least 30 feet or more above me. The entire vault and many of the angled walls soaring upward were black from the soot of fires that had clearly burned here for some time. Maybe years. Maybe centuries.

And this was definitely the same cave that I'd been photographing. I had studied the cave at the start of the assignment. I knew its shape and outline.

Imagining a bird's-eye view from above, it was like a long, skinny hourglass on its side with a pinch point—where the space between the walls narrowed—about 25 yards back from the entrance. And we were now in the inner part of the hourglass.

But something was off.

I quickly realized I was seeing the cave walls from a lower position. There was rock exposed that I'd never seen before.

I must have looked silly with my mouth open because Wren was soon at my side, smiling. Crouching on the cave's packed-dirt floor, he made a motion with his hand and was quickly joined by one of his people. They spoke to each other as they examined my injury.

It suddenly registered that the other person—if *person* was the right word—was a woman. At first, it was hard to tell, but her breasts mounded the animal skin she wore. And her voice was pitched slightly higher. She also had blue eyes—clear, bright, luminous—and a backward-sloping face. And tangled hair the same color as Wren's.

The woman started to reach out to touch my wetsuit but Wren slapped her hand away and spoke angrily to her, his voice echoing in the cave.

She scowled and spat out her own jangling words in defiance.

He smiled and patted her knee several times. Were they husband and wife? Something else?

The woman's actions reminded me of the diamond ring hanging from my neck.

With the heat from the fire, I didn't need the wetsuit so I took it off with some difficulty and set it next to me. I then took hold of the ring in my right hand. Its hard surface was a comfort.

As I massaged the ring with my fingers, both Wren and the woman leaned forward to get a better view. Suddenly remembering that this was the same ring on the skeleton's hand in the same cave, I lifted it from my chest and extended it toward them so they could see it better.

At the same moment, another man appeared over us. He barked something and grabbed the woman under the arm and started pulling her away.

Wren jumped to his feet, shouted out, and pushed the man with one hand at the same time he broke the man's grip on the woman with the other.

The new man—as strong as Wren—moved his eyes from me to Wren and back. Then, in one quick movement, he scooped up my wetsuit, turned, and threw it into the fire.

Wren yelled and charged the man, and they were soon on the floor grappling with each other while the woman stood screaming at both of them.

Confused by what had just happened, I watched the wetsuit hiss and start to melt in the flames. Then I turned to look at the other people crowded around the fire. All of them were silently staring at my burning wetsuit and ignoring the fighting men.

An eerie feeling swept over me. It reminded me of an earlier chapter in my life when I helped produce video games. And learned about the "Uncanny Valley." The uneasy feeling of seeing a creation that was almost human, but not quite. Where something was slightly off. Something familiar but also alien at the same time.

It was starting to make sense. I had read enough time-travel stories to be familiar with the basics of a "multiverse" that had many worlds running alongside ours. Including the past. And that someone might be able to travel to another "timestream" given the right conditions or technology. Or maybe just slip back in time on the same stream without jumping across space-time continuums.

The world of science and rationality, of course, rejected all this and said it was impossible to travel back through time. Yet, here I was.

I had apparently found a portal to another universe or time period. A rabbit hole to the past.

I leaned back on my elbows and followed a spark from the fire as it rose up into the gloom of the cave's upper reaches, where I could swear I heard bats squeaking.

I lowered my head to look again at the group gathered around the fire.

My God. They really *were* Neanderthals. *Homo neanderthalensis.*

I—a *Homo sapiens* member—had traveled back in time.

PART TWO

The Stranger

9

Dr. Victoria Busher pulled out her magnifier and crouched down to study the skeletal hand again.

They had brushed away more of the sand and sediment, and she'd sent the volunteers off to work in other parts of the cave. She wanted to examine the hand on her own.

Incredibly, it was whole. All 27 bones were intact and well preserved. There didn't appear to be any post-depositional activity from animal or worm burrowing.

And then there was the ring.

She reached out to touch it with her hand inside a surgical glove. She felt the curve of the band, the prong of the setting, and finally, the sharp edges of the center stone.

A gold ring with a diamond. Astonishing. Like

nothing she'd ever seen or even heard of in an archaeological context. If this didn't cinch her tenure position at U.T., she didn't know what would.

But she had to see this through to completion. There could be no mistakes. No questions about authenticity. She had to carefully follow the normal steps of an excavation. Methods and process. No shortcuts.

And no room for emotional entanglements of the type Tom presented. No more wanting to touch him or have him touch her. She would keep her distance. Keep it professional.

The osteoarchaeologist from the Spanish government had already tested the soil samples and was now waiting for his English counterpart to arrive from London. Because this was Gibraltar, British procedures had to be followed. Lots of forms to fill out.

The guidelines for handling or removing human remains were specific and strict. This was, after all, a burial site.

And there was the museum director to deal with.

Because the museum was partially funding the dig, he wanted the hand and ring to end up on display inside the museum. Victoria preferred temporarily removing the remains for recording and testing, then replacing them, with the aim of eventually having an elaborate in situ *display inside the cave itself.*

It would be an ongoing battle.

In the meantime, she still worried about Tom. She hadn't heard from him since that unusual call on

Saturday. She hoped he wasn't sinking into depression or worse.

But she worried about the dig and her career more.

10

I had misjudged the situation. What I'd interpreted as two men fighting over the woman for some perceived slight was not that at all.

After they'd rolled around on the ground and scuffled with each other for a few minutes, they both broke into hysterical laughter. And the whole assemblage around the fire joined in.

Wren then jumped to his feet and extended a hand to his adversary and pulled him up. They both walked over to the woman and dipped their heads to her.

She put her hands to their shoulders and pushed them back, raising her voice. She was angry. Or so I believed. Until her tight mouth relaxed into a broad smile and she giggled.

It was as if I'd been watching an act play out on

stage, then the actors applaud each other for their performances when the scene breaks. I was confused and made a mental note to figure out what I'd just witnessed.

But that would have to wait because I was immediately confronted by a man who had shuffled over and now squatted in front of me, examining me and my leg wound.

He was definitely older. A quick glance around the group told me he was the oldest one there. An elder or a leader, I thought.

Four large feathers hung from his hair, and he had a leather necklace holding several animal claws and talons. They rattled and bounced against his bony chest as he prodded my leg with his fingers and mumbled to himself.

Looking more closely, I saw that not all of the man's fingers were there. Several were stumped at the first or second joint. And with skin hanging loosely from his heavily scarred arms and torso, he looked emaciated.

But he didn't look unhappy. In fact, it was the opposite. He was grinning from ear to ear.

After he said something over his head to the others, he leaned forward to study me, his gaze darting from body part to body part. When his dark eyes met mine, he widened his smile and raised an open hand to his face, stroking it from his cheeks down to his neck.

He repeated this movement several times while saying the same words. *Minya, minya* is how they sounded to me.

I had no idea what that meant but I didn't feel danger coming from this man nor anyone else in the group. I got the sense that I was a pleasant surprise to them. Almost a welcome guest. But why were they so accepting of me? I was an outsider. Different. Maybe because I was exotic. Like one of the monkeys that were an ancient feature of Gibraltar.

I soon had two women attending to my leg, one rubbing off the poultice, the other cleaning the wound with water she dripped from a large gourd. Then they both blew on the wound with their warm breath until it was dry.

The bleeding had stopped, and so had the pain and dizziness. I felt like I was on the way to recovery from the hyena attack. That was the good news.

The bad was that I was foggy about how I had gotten to this place and time. From the archeological record, I knew that Neanderthals had lived in Eurasia for almost four hundred thousand years. So when was this? And even more importantly, how was I going to get home?

◆ ◆

The plan was simple. Stay with these people while my leg healed. Try not to antagonize anyone. Be friendly. Don't provoke. Then get back to the cairn and the lake and do my best to reverse engineer what I'd done to get here.

Based on what I remembered from my EMT class, it would be about a week of keeping the wound clean and dry, then another week or two for scabbing and final healing. And if I needed to shortcut that timeline, so be it. There were hospitals where I'd come from.

And while I was here, observe everything I could.

As mind-bending as all this was, it was also a monumental opportunity to capture real-world experience from a bygone age. There were entire fields of study devoted to how humans came to be. Most projected back from excavated artifacts and fossilized bone fragments. Inferences. Deductions. Theories and guesses.

The debates among archeologists, anthropologists, biologists, and more recently, geneticists, were long and legendary. Mainly because no one really *knew* what had caused the species *Homo sapiens*—us—to ultimately rule the planet and leave other competing *Hominini* contenders on history's scrapheap.

Victoria had explained to me that at different points in the distant past there were several human-like species that existed on earth at the same time. And for one reason or another, we Sapiens had ended up on top.

Now here I was, actually *in* that past. Living it. Seeing it firsthand.

It would create a sensation. The scientific world would go into a frenzy and I'd be able to write my own ticket. Books, documentaries, consulting with museums ... I could capitalize on this fluke.

This could change my life.

But I was getting ahead of myself. I wasn't thinking about those closest to me: Carolyn and our unborn baby. I was still hoping they'd been found. They were my family now and I wanted to be back with them—or their memories, at least.

As hard as it was to admit, I had to assume they weren't alive. But I wasn't forgetting them. The heartache was too fresh.

It was just that all of this was so extraordinary, so unbelievable. My thinking was off balance. I had to settle down and get back in control.

But first I wanted to sleep. It had been a long, tiring day. And as if my thoughts were being read, I was soon hopping on one leg, arms around Wren and his competitor-friend on each side, being led to another chamber behind the fire. Dark and low-ceilinged, it was filled with piled-up furs and animal skins.

As Wren lowered me down onto a thick fur, I realized that this was their sleeping area.

While I arranged myself on the soft pelt—pulling over another skin as a blanket—others in the group started to filter in, finding their own spots around me. The musky smell of body odors mingled with those of the animal hides and smoke, but it wasn't unpleasant. And I felt oddly secure in the middle of these strange people.

Once all the moving and murmuring had stopped, I felt my body sinking while I watched flickers of orange light from the fire dance on the cave walls.

Then I heard it.

It started quietly, like a low hum, first coming from one side of me and then the other. Soon, the sound of voices rose in time to a synchronized rhythm. They were singing together!

It wasn't loud. More like a low chant. But definitely a communal song.

The entire cave was filled with a vocal pulse that gathered in energy until it finally reached a peak. Then it started a slow drift back down, and the chorus of voices faded away into silence.

I was mesmerized and soon lost to sleep.

11

I spent the next week trying to learn as much as I could about these Neanderthals. My leg was healing well and I was starting to walk on it.

They gave me an animal hide—deer, it looked like—to wear as a kind of cape or mantle over my shorts. I thought it would be itchy or hard against the skin but it was soft and pliant from years of use. The smell wasn't strong, and this turned out to be a flexible garment I could wear in different ways depending on my activity.

It was warm enough inside the cave. And on my first forays outside, I could generate enough heat as long as I kept moving. But always with my hide cape.

The only things I really missed were shoes. I could probably make a pair if I stayed long enough, but I was hoping I wouldn't need to. This was going to be a temporary visit.

And I wished I had a way to record what I was seeing. A camera. Or even just something to write with. As flabbergasted as I was with this situation, the journalist in me was ready to do his job. Notice and document. Get down to business.

Of course, writing had yet to be invented. There was no paper and no efficient writing tool. There were feathers that I could fashion into quills, but there was no ink. I would have to rely on my memory until I figured out something else.

One thing I could do while waiting for my leg to mend was learn their language. Communication was key to understanding these people and their alien world.

And I was confident in calling them *people* because that's what they were. Part of the genus *Homo*. The evolutionary cousins of Sapiens. Like us. Not the dim-witted knuckle-draggers usually depicted in the general media but thinking, feeling people. Who, I now knew, sang and spoke.

Even if I was only staying for a short time, I had to communicate with them to truly grasp what I was dealing with in what I now guessed was around 40,000 years ago, or 40 kya in scientific lingo. It was a wild guess, sure, but I had to start somewhere.

So I began with the small group I was closest to: Wren, the old man, and the woman with the jarring voice. Others, especially children, were curious and wandered over to us, but they bored quickly and left. I focused my attention on these three.

First, names.

With the four of us sitting together near the fire after an evening meal of roasted roots and pine nuts, I touched a finger to my chest and said my name slowly.

"Tom Cook."

Looking at each person in turn, I repeated my name three times.

Nothing.

I gestured at Wren and poked my finger in his direction several times.

"What is name?" I asked, raising my eyebrows and tilting my head in a way I thought would indicate a question.

Nothing.

This confirmed my suspicion. With a couple of exceptions, few seemed to have personal names of their own, using either tone or pitch or something else to call to each other. Or, at least, I couldn't discern their names. So I would give them my own nicknames.

I had a thought.

I pointed to myself and said my name again.

Then I signaled to Wren and instructed, "Make this sound: *Rrrr*."

I held the sound while I touched my mouth. *"Rrrr."*

Wren finally nodded and made a tentative but passable version of the sound in a nasal voice, like a young child with a cold.

I smiled and gave him a thumbs-up sign, which he tried to repeat with a puzzled look on his face.

I laughed and shook my head.

They all laughed and shook their heads, too.

Well, that was something. They understood mimicry.

Next, I said to Wren, pointing once more to my mouth: *"Ennn."* I extended the final consonant, raising my eyebrows again.

Wren did not disappoint and made the sound of *innn*. Close enough.

I tapped my mouth and drew out the combined sounds: *"Rrrr - ennn."*

Then I repeated them faster. *Rr-en. Rr-en.* Wren.

I gestured to him. "Now you."

He glanced at the others then back to me and touched his chest. *"Rr-in,"* he said with confidence. *"Rr-in."*

I smiled and nodded my head. He had it.

Then I patted my chest and raised my eyebrows and shoulders in question.

He didn't hesitate. *"Tum kuk,"* he said boldly.

I had broken through.

And I didn't miss the look the woman gave me. It was a look I'd seen before.

◆ ◆

A couple of days later and another revelation.

After a full day of gathering firewood outside the

cave—with me tagging along and testing my scabbed leg—I found myself sitting and observing a small group around the cave's central fire busy with toolmaking. In this case, stone cutting tools, the highest-tech objects of this primitive world.

With two of them roasting pieces of rabbit on sticks over the fire, the others were striking and hammering away at rocks. They were making handaxes—the sharp-edged, multi-purpose, cutting tools that were knapped into shape to fit comfortably in the hand. The handaxe was a pivotal step in human evolution. The tool was used for butchering animals and for flaking off blades for weaponry.

While I had read articles and studies on how the different stone-knapping and blade-flaking methods had evolved over the millennia, including the subtle differences between the Levallois technique versus the Acheulian, what was even more interesting to me was the way the group interacted. And more generally, how they organized themselves socially.

There didn't seem to be obvious nuclear families. Instead of a singular husband, wife, and child or children, what I saw was more open and fluid. One study I'd read suggested that Neanderthals practiced Polygyny, or two women for each man. This seemed possible, but it wasn't the only option I was seeing.

I looked over to Wren, who was cleaving off thin flakes of quartz from a rounded stone core. The woman who sat next to him was the mother of his son, who was playing with other children on the other side of the fire.

There was another woman near Wren. I'd learned she was the mother of an infant daughter who sat next to her and cheerfully occupied herself by hitting two stones together. But this woman had also mothered another child by a different man, also busy flaking off razor-sharp blades nearby.

So while these were not monogamous families in the same way we moderns thought of them, there was the impression of a loving and supportive relationship among all the individuals.

Which was night and day compared to my younger years of family life.

My mother died early of cancer, and my father was a drunk who left me solo to bounce from one foster home to another, where I was regularly beaten and exposed to other forms of abuse. I was a living punching bag, apparently born to passively receive the violence and aggression of adults.

I was bitter and selfish early on. Walled off from others who were supposed to be close to me. I didn't trust them and I retreated into myself. Alone against the world. Until Carolyn.

By contrast, my Neanders—this was my new familiar term for them—all seemed to care for each other across the board, regardless of family unit. They were kind-hearted and, outside of their play-acting, gentle. And their culture was already having an impact on me.

My Obsessive Compulsive Disorder behaviors were already lessening. I sensed my constant need for order and control softening. I wasn't checking and rechecking things as much. This led to the happy effect of my having fewer attacks of panic, vertigo, and claustrophobia, which I'd always blamed on my OCD.

My self-serving bitterness, earned like a merit badge over many years of fighting against family and society, was easing around these people.

Musing on all this, I felt the call of nature and walked outside the cave to pee. My peaceful enjoyment of the moment—the cool night air and the appetizing smell of cooking meat—was interrupted by Wren, who must have had the same idea and was suddenly standing next to me. And I mean, *right* next to me.

"Excuse me," I said, sidestepping a couple of paces in mid-stream. He was invading my personal space.

"*Tum kuk,*" he said proudly, flashing a wide smile and staring at my penis.

I immediately lost the biological urge.

"*Rr-in,*" he said decisively, lifting his much thicker penis in an unselfconscious way that surprised me.

For them, shame and embarrassment were not emotions to be concerned with.

12

I was near the end of my recuperation time when the old man—I called him Grandpa—handed me a lighted torch and invited me to follow him. We ended up in a side chamber or gallery of the cave that was connected to the main space by a short passageway. I had never noticed this area in Present Dig Time, as I now called my prior life. Maybe a rockslide had covered it up in the ensuing millennia.

And *gallery* was the right word because once I stopped and waved the torch in front of a smooth wall, I was stunned.

During my research, I had read that Neanderthals created virtually no art. Yes, there'd been a few discoveries of crude etchings or possible pigment splatters, but there were no sophisticated drawings of animals like those found in the famous caves of Lascaux and Altamira. Those were linked to post-Neanderthal people.

It was generally thought that the higher symbolic arts—painting, pottery, ornamental jewelry—had been achieved only by modern humans—Sapiens.

Yet here I was standing in front of a wall filled with all kinds of art.

There were negative hand stencils where someone had loaded up a pipe or their cheeks with watery pigment and blown the mixture over an outstretched hand placed against the wall, and then removed it.

I also saw simple etchings where someone had rubbed a stone over the hard rock many times to make deep grooves. These markings made configurations of lines, circles, squares, and even combinations that looked like tic-tac-toe designs.

And then there were the paintings. One large, complex composition caught my attention. It looked like a meeting scene with two distinct groups of people. The colors varied from red to brown and black. Probably made from ochre, mud, and charcoal.

Moving my torch closer, I gestured to the simple figures in one group that appeared stockier. Although they were colored with different pigments, overall they seemed lighter in tone compared to the other group.

"Looks more like you," I said, turning and pointing to Grandpa.

He smiled knowingly.

I turned back to the painting and nodded at the other figures represented. They were more slender. And the colors were darker overall, although there was a range of light to dark.

I tapped my chest with my finger.

"More like me."

The man moved his eyes from me to the painting and back again. He nodded while saying something quickly. Then he made the same downward, pinching hand movement on his face, repeating the words again: "Minya, minya."

Now I understood. And had more reason to believe in my 40 kya estimate of the time period.

His group had interacted with a group of Sapiens, who were the darker, slimmer figures. And this made sense.

Supposedly, the last wave of anatomically modern humans—*H. sapiens*—only arrived in western Europe from Africa approximately 45,000 or so years ago, where Neanderthals had been living for hundreds of thousands of years. The Neanderthals—at least some of them—had evolved their lighter skin pigmentation to match the higher latitudes and the resulting decrease in crucial sunlight that helped form Vitamin D in the skin. The newcomers, the Sapiens, had not had enough time for natural selection to do its work.

And the confusion I saw in Grandpa's face came from the fact that I wasn't dark-skinned. Although tanned from all my outdoor activities, I was a modern white man. And thin. Or, using the official anthropological word, *gracile*.

But now I wondered if it was really his people who had made these paintings. Maybe it was the Sapiens who had picked up the charcoal and ochre pigments in the cave to do it.

Grandpa must have read my mind because I watched him walk over to a dark corner and come back with a burned and blackened stick. He stepped to the wall and started filling in what was clearly an unfinished figure on the far side of the painting.

No, it was this group—or their ancestors—who had created this prehistoric art.

After Grandpa finished his painting, we walked back to the main chamber in silence. My head was spinning. Now I could add representational art to my Neanderthal discoveries.

I had to bring all this new information forward to my time.

◆ ◆

I had decided. Today was the day I was going back.

The sun hadn't risen but the sky was already brightening from the east. I sat outside the cave entrance and rubbed a hand over my leg. Not all of the scab had fallen off, but the wound was healed enough, and the leg was strong from my having used it each day.

I hadn't said any goodbyes. I struggled with this

decision but finally concluded there was no easy way to do this. What was I going to say? That I had to get back to the future? That I needed to exploit this accident of time?

It was simpler just to be gone.

Maybe I was letting them down, but that was nothing new for me. I had disappointed plenty of people in my life with my self-interests.

I started down the slope to the lake wearing only my shorts and the skin mantle over the ring that hung around my neck. I had a small pouch of evidence—the end of Grandpa's painting stick—tucked in my pocket, and I carried a small stone blade for protection. I hoped I wouldn't need it.

I reached the lake and the cairn just as the sun peeked over the mountains around Algiers in the distance. The sky was smeared with high clouds, and although the air was wintry crisp, my pushed pace put a rim of sweat on my forehead.

After some searching, I found my mask and fins at the base of the cairn, but the snorkel and headlamp were gone. Carolyn's iPhone, too. Probably picked up by someone, or maybe an animal, and carried away. No matter. I had what I needed. And if some future archeologist puzzled over finding the corroded parts of a smartphone, I didn't care. I was going home.

Standing at the water's edge, I looked up toward the Rock. I could make out the line of caves that would one day be famous around the world as the last refuge of the Neanderthals.

Feelings of fondness mixed with images of contented people sitting around a fire living their simple lives one day at a time. Unselfishly depending on each other for their common good. Things certainly missing in my life.

A life I needed to get back to.

It was time.

I threw off the mantle, put on my fins and mask, and stepped into the cold water. Hopefully, I wouldn't be cold for long.

I splashed brackish water on my face and pushed off into an easy swim.

After a minute or so I turned onto my back and kept kicking. Gauging by the angles with the cairn and the opposite lakeshore, I finally stopped, bent at the waist, lifted one leg, and headed down into the water's gloom.

Trying to clear my mind of all thoughts and worries, my senses focused on the pressure of the water against my skin. I needed to find the portal from one time to the other. The rabbit hole that would transport me back from 40,000 years ago to 2019.

After clearing my ears, I stopped descending and righted myself. Hanging in the water column like a jellyfish, I closed my eyes and waited.

And waited.

Feeling the cold penetrating into my core, I gave a gentle kick and began slowly floating back up to the surface. Ready for the shift. For the rippling. For the peculiar groaning that would mark the transition.

But nothing happened.

I opened my eyes and broke the surface. Lifting my mask and spinning around in a full circle, I was dismayed to see the dry, spiraled cairn and the sloped plain leading up to the Rock. Nothing had changed.

I had failed.

13

After hours of retrying, moving this way and that around the lake, and getting more and more frustrated and frantic each time, I finally gave up.

The sun was well past its high point, and a flock of pelicans now crowded the top of the cairn. They were squawking and surely laughing at the stupid human who was repeating his curious actions again and again for no apparent reason.

What those birds didn't see was the panic building inside of me. Sitting back on shore, I put my head between my legs and concentrated on quieting myself by tapping my chest in rhythm with my shallow and erratic breathing.

Now what? Was I stuck here forever in 40 kya? Living in a cave with a bunch of Neanderthals?

Admittedly, nice Neanderthals that I liked. But still, I was trapped in the past. The Paleolithic past.

There had to be a way out of this. *Think!*

Leaving my fins and mask, I put on my deerskin top and started a slow walk back toward the cave retracing in my mind what I had done that first time with Santiago. There was something I was missing. Something I hadn't done right this time. What was it?

As I shuffled over a sand dune, I came to a stop and crouched down, picking up a handful of sun-warmed sand. I let it slip out between my fingers.

Sand. Beach. Miami Beach. Yes!

Closing my eyes, I let my mind recreate an old memory from childhood. When, during a horrible stint in a foster home in Miami, I would escape the family's screaming and turmoil...

"Where's Tom?" I heard my foster father yell out, slapping the belt in his hand.

Knowing what was coming, I jumped into the deep end of our filthy backyard pool. It was full of leaves and algae, but I paid no attention.

"Come here!" he said, drunk and angry at the pool's edge. "Get out of there."

"No!" I answered and sank to the bottom where I sat for as long as I could hold out.

The utter silence and peace of being underwater would form the basis of my dreams of being transported to another—better—life. Where I wasn't constantly beaten and yelled at.

The pool was my safe haven. The water. The shells ... Wait!

I remembered that I always held a seashell in one hand when I dove to the bottom of that pool. It had become a habit. The shells somehow linked me to a different world. A more ancient world.

So it wasn't just being submerged that provided the environment for my escapes into my dream fantasies. It was also the totemic influence of the shells.

I thought back to that first dive with Santiago. What had I done differently? What was my totem?

I saw it immediately. It was the diamond ring. I had rubbed the ring on its necklace but forgotten to do the same this last time. That was the difference.

The ring itself was my connection to the past and the rawhide shoelace holding it—that I had bought in a shop in Gibraltar—my link to the present. The ring and necklace I still wore.

I reached up and pushed it against my chest as a confirmation.

Standing, I looked toward the lake and then up to the low sun. It was too late to try again, and I was worn out. But I would attempt it again soon.

Next time, I would make it back to 2019.

◆ ◆

I needed to recover from my dashed diving hopes, and I was asked the following day to join another outdoor excursion. It would provide a distraction from my failed effort and hopefully give me more insight into this world I would soon leave.

I'd been patiently spending more time around the fire trying to learn their language while also inserting mine. *Cave. Fire. Food. Outside.* Combining simple words with lots of pantomiming usually got the idea across. It was getting easier to communicate.

It was just four of us, and we walked down into an area of sand dunes southeast of the cave entrance, the Rock looming over our backs.

There was a snap to the mid-morning air that was hard to describe. Not exactly cold, but not warm either. A brisk tingling on the skin. Like what mountain air feels like, but here at sea level. Unfamiliar but electrifying at the same time.

We were on what appeared to be a hunting or gathering trip, although how much of it was for my benefit was hard to decipher. I noticed that they watched my reactions every time we came upon an unusual plant or heard the fleeing sounds of an unseen animal in the underbrush.

Leading the group was Wren, who wore only his loincloth and carried a long, wooden spear with an attached blade in one hand. Next came the same woman who I now knew was his sister. I named her Brassy for her piercing voice and strident manner.

Brassy was short and muscular, somewhere around five foot one. She wore a necklace of pierced shells over her simple hide tunic, and she had a large, woven pouch slung over her right shoulder. She was focused and keenly aware of her surroundings, constantly moving her head left and right to take it all in.

There was something visceral about Brassy. Animalistic. Sly. Almost catlike.

She intrigued me.

Also along was Brassy's young son. I guessed him to be about five years old.

Completely naked, the boy had a permanent wild-eyed look on his face, and his long brown hair swept up and back off his head like he'd been sitting in front of a large fan. He held a miniature version of Wren's spear and constantly raised it to his head looking for something to throw it at.

It turned out that Brassy was a widow. The father had been attacked and dragged off by a leopard soon after the boy's birth. The boy didn't have a nickname yet.

I pulled up the rear, trying my best to keep pace. It was hard without shoes, struggling to avoid rocks and dried brambles with my civilized, soft feet.

We dropped down into a shallow gully lined with cork oak and wild olive trees. As soon as we reached a thicket at the bottom, a flock of quail exploded into the sky and veered off to the north. At the same time, several rabbits dashed in front of us trying to flee.

Wren shouted something and the boy threw his spear in the rabbits' general direction, hitting nothing.

But Wren had launched his spear at the same time and it skewered the biggest of the rabbits against the side of the gully. Considering the speed of the rabbit and the weight of the wooden spear, it was an impressive show of hunting skill.

Brassy quickly pounced on the rabbit, pulled it off the spear tip, and smacked it against the nearest tree to make sure it was dead. Then she slipped it into her pouch with a look of pride.

"*Ah-o-o-o!*" they all shouted simultaneously three times in a row. Triumph. I joined them on the last one to their amused satisfaction.

We spent the slow return trip starting and stopping. Wren and Brassy inspected rotting logs to find grubs and dig in the sandy soil for roots of various descriptions. All went into the pouch that was soon full and heavy.

Rabbit—that's what I decided to call him—used his boundless energy to chase after every rabbit, bird, and mouse that skittered away from us on the rolling savannah.

We were almost home when an older boy suddenly appeared in front of us, tears lining his cheeks. He spoke rapidly and we were soon on a dead run up the slope toward the cave.

Watching the rigid faces of Wren and Brassy, I knew that something terrible had happened.

◆ ◆

The cave was in turmoil. Women wailed and children cried over several bodies lying on the ground, either dead or severely injured. All adult men.

There had been an attack on the group. And the injuries looked like stab wounds. Deep cuts into flesh that was either bleeding or had already bled out, leaving pools of it on the dirt floor.

The smell of sweat mixing with blood was everywhere in the cave, especially in the main chamber with the fire. The head of one unfortunate man had been pulled out of the flames, and the metallic smell coming from its blistered skin was nauseating.

I tried to figure out what had happened, going first to Wren. But he was beside himself with anger and what looked like fear to me. Apparently, his wife—if that's what she was—and his young daughter had been taken. Kidnapped.

Brassy was busy helping with the injured so I approached Grandpa, who stood against a rock wall, tears dripping off his stubbled chin. He wasn't injured. Probably not worth the attackers' effort.

"What happened?" I asked him, raising my hands and shoulders.

He shook his head side to side. "Minya," he said over and over.

Grandpa stared at me for a long time, his eyes narrowing. Then he lifted his right hand and pushed a finger against my chest. "Minya."

It was a simple statement but with a deep undertone

of sadness and disappointment. Then he turned and walked away.

As I watched him join a small group attending to an injured—but still living—man, I suddenly realized that he was linking me to this.

I was the Minya.

14

The communal singing had finished echoing through the cave when Wren approached me.

The injured were being cared for, and the two dead men had been moved out of the main chamber. Blood still marked the floor, but Grandpa was busy covering every trace of it with sand. The smell of death had dissipated, replaced by the normal one of wood smoke.

Wren's face showed his anguish. His mouth was turned down but his eyes flashed rage above the dried tears.

He grabbed my arm at the same time he jerked his head and started pulling me. *Puk* was the word I heard him say. Probably *come*. There was a matter-of-factness to his voice. I was expecting hostility for my perceived involvement, but it wasn't that. It was more like determination. I followed him to the gallery chamber.

We both stood in front of the large painting, him holding the torch close, me wondering what he was going to do. I anticipated blame and was prepared for something even worse: violence.

Instead, Wren surprised me. With his right hand, he patted the Sapien group on the wall. Then he moved the same hand to me and gently placed it over my heart. He pressed and looked imploringly into my eyes.

"*Uwa,*" he said in a quiet voice. "*Uwa.*"

I didn't know the word, but I could sense its meaning. He wanted me to help. But how?

He sank to the ground on his knees and motioned for me to do the same.

Grabbing a nearby stick he drew a diagram in the dirt: a circle on the left, a circle on the right. He pitted the left circle with marks from the tip of the stick then pointed it at the wall painting. "Minya," he said. The attackers.

Moving to the right circle, he drew a smaller circle inside of it. "*Nosi,*" he said solemnly. Their group. Now smaller.

I had read enough Neanderthal research to know that one of the proposed reasons for their extinction was their small group or clan size. Larger groups can generate more ideas and solutions to problems. The bigger the group, the more ideas. More "networked intelligence," as the academic papers put it.

And now I noticed something on the wall painting

I had missed before.

The Sapiens group was larger. If the art accurately depicted the meeting of the two groups, then these Neanderthals had the smaller number. Which now created a bigger long-term problem because this band—my group—was now down two female members.

And I got the distinct feeling that Wren intuitively understood this and was now communicating that concern to me with his smaller circle.

Wren then drew a thick line from the small circle to the larger Sapien one. I was so taken aback to see his use of symbolism with pictorial shapes and lines that I almost overlooked him making a single mark in the dirt outside the small circles.

He pointed at me. Then he put his finger on the isolated mark.

He said, *"Te,"* or something similar. *You*, no doubt.

Then he dragged his finger from my mark and stopped it inside the smallest circle. The message was clear: He wanted me to join them.

I was another man. Even if I wasn't adept in their ways, I had the most unique talent of all: I was a *Homo sapiens*. A "wise man" by scientific classification. I was like the abductors. A Minya. I was their secret weapon.

But to do what?

Somehow knowing my question, Wren held up his hand with two fingers extended. Then he covered the fingers with his other hand and pulled them in close to his chest.

I realized he wanted my help to go after the kidnappers. To rescue the captives. And captives they surely were. Females were too valuable to kill.

He gave me an awkward big-toothed smile and raised his thick eyebrows. He was waiting for my answer.

There were two problems with this idea. First, by taking action in this prehistoric world, how would I be affecting the future? Would the tiniest alteration caused by me ripple down through the centuries and millennia?

This was the famous "butterfly effect" of chaos theory, first suggested by MIT professor Edward Lorenz back in the 1960s. Where the smallest change in one state—like the flapping of a single butterfly's wings—can result in large differences to a later state—say, the creation of a tornado thousands of miles away.

If I joined this rescue effort, I would be taking an active role in the past. I wouldn't be just innocently observing from the sidelines. I would be affecting things. I would take part. I would become an actor on the stage. A player with the potential to influence the future.

I might be a butterfly.

The second worry was even more immediate. I was planning to retrace my time-travel steps to get back to 2019. I had already failed once, but I was anxious to try again.

Yet part of me hesitated.

The reality was: I liked these people. And I'd become

strangely invested in their fate. I didn't want them to disappear or die out in the way that all the history books and articles claimed.

I was oddly rooting for them. For their caring, harmonious lifestyle. A manner of living that was now acutely affected by an outside group. A group pressing violence. A violence I knew something about.

I decided right then that I would delay—only temporarily—the next attempt to get back to my world. Instead, I would help the Neanderthals.

We would try to save the two captives together.

◆ ◆

The first thing we needed was a plan. My specialty.

The Minyas were right now dragging two of Wren's family to who-knows-where, and we had lost a lot of time. It was now the end of the day we'd arrived back at the cave.

A group of four of us—me plus Wren and two more of their strongest men—sat in a small circle next to the fire. Grandpa hovered over Wren's shoulder, and Brassy and three other women and their children stood nearby, watching and listening intently.

Using lots of signing and gesturing, it was decided that we four would pursue the kidnappers and try to rescue the captives. The others—the women, children, and Grandpa—would stay behind, with more men ready to protect them and continue with the burials, hunting, and whatever else the home group required.

But something else was needed.

I'd read that a key to human evolution was the emergence of forward planning. The ability to anticipate a future situation and then imagine the steps needed to bring that state into being. Like heating bark to make the tar to attach—or haft—a stone tip to a spear.

And that required larger brains to do the mental processing involved.

Neanderthals had those big brains. On par with—and in some cases even larger than—modern human brains. But I saw a subtle underdevelopment in forward planning with my Neanders.

I'd earlier noticed a lot of joking and ribbing around the fire about accidents and problems with their annual gathering of birds' eggs each summer.

White storks bred and laid their eggs in May or June in marshy wetlands on the coastal plain surrounding the Rock. From conversations overheard plus some additional questioning, I discovered that raiding these nutritious egg clutches was a time-honored tradition with the Neanders.

They'd learned how to anticipate the birds' arrival from Africa, but they were inefficient in retrieving the eggs. They didn't prepare for the worst-case scenarios.

There was a lot of fun-poking at one of the men who had slipped or fallen during a rainstorm, breaking all the eggs he carried in one of their simple pouches. Apparently, it wasn't an isolated incident. There had been a lot of egg accidents like this.

Not only had they not thought to divide the precious eggs among several people to minimize the risk, but their pouches weren't good at protecting the eggs. What they needed was the equivalent of the modern egg carton, with individual compartments for each egg.

It was a simple enough idea, easily constructed by, say, tying birds' nests together, clam-shell style. But when I suggested it, I was told that they preferred how they had always gathered their eggs. If someone fell and smashed the eggs, it was meant to be. The will of the animal spirits or something like that.

To be fair, I had no reason to believe that the Sapiens of this time were any better at this sort of anticipatory thinking. Maybe worse. And maybe it took another 40,000 years or so to improve on and develop this cognitive capacity.

So I wasn't assigning blame. But there were consequences from this limited capability in forward planning.

They could make simple plans, but chasing after a hostile group and hoping to bring back the kidnapees—or what was left of them—was a higher order of complexity. And right up my alley.

◆ ◆

The main thing to figure out was where the abductors were heading so we could start the pursuit.

After acting out my question to the group while interjecting keywords like *Where?* and *How far?*, one of the other men started pumping his hand up and down. I instantly nicknamed him Hand, nodded to him, and listened closely.

With help from the others, I learned that Hand had originally come to the cave from the far north. He had been part of a trade with another group that acquired a female in exchange. This was the kind of bargaining used to increase genetic diversity that seemed hard-wired into the brains of all members of the *Homo* genus.

If there weren't enough female or male prospects of child-bearing or child-creating age around, you went outside the group to find them. By peaceful means or otherwise.

But the key point for me was that Hand had come from the north. With more questioning, I determined that his homeland was on Spain's central plateau, somewhere to the west of present-day Madrid. And he had heard plenty of stories in his earlier life that this was also the land of the Minyas.

This matched exactly with what I'd learned about the spread of early humans westward to the Iberian Peninsula.

Spain's high tablelands defined the southern limit of the steppe-tundra landscape of the Upper Paleolithic era. This was the dry, cold expanse created by the low temperatures of the Ice Age, for which Neanderthals were well suited. It was the land of the wooly mammoth, rhino, reindeer, bison, and antelope that one usually associated with Eurasia's periods of glaciation.

This was where we were going. North.

I was continually surprised by how similar the overall climate was in 40 kya Gibraltar compared to 2019. I had read this fact somewhere but still expected to see wooly mammoths every time I stepped outside the cave. Instead, the weather was—thankfully—about the same. But we were going to leave that behind. Which meant planning for cold had to be added to the list of preparations.

I drew my checklist right on the dirt floor with a sharpened stick. Using crude pictographs, I made what were basically bullet-point lines representing the items we needed to gather for the journey.

For weapons, I sketched images of spears and clubs. For cold-weather clothes, I drew mantles, robes, and leggings. Next was a line for the stone cutting tools that could double as knapped flakes for butchering and for weaponry.

For traveling food, I created a simple head with an open mouth and an arrow pointing to it. They would know what to bring.

Finally, I laid down a small block of the dark manganese dioxide that they scraped from and mixed with wood chips for fire-making.

I looked at my floor list with satisfaction and scanned the surrounding faces. I saw mostly bewilderment, but Wren was smiling and nodding. He understood.

Almost immediately, he was barking out orders and people were running off in different directions to gather the needed supplies.

Within minutes, a collection of tools and provisions mounded up next to the floor list. We'd be ready to start the next morning.

As we stood to move to the sleeping chamber, Rabbit suddenly ran to me with his hair flying and hugged my legs. Surprised, I almost fell over, but Brassy was there to hold me up and keep me standing.

I picked Rabbit up and lifted him to me. He put his little arms around my neck and squeezed. I held him out and glanced at his mother. Her face was as soft as I'd ever seen it, and she fixed me with a look. The same look Carolyn often gave me.

It was an unmistakable look of affection.

15

We started out just after sunrise.

By my guess, it was early November, and the morning was clear and cool as the four of us—Wren, Hand, me, and another I named Shorty for obvious reasons—started trekking north along the base of the Rock.

Earlier, there'd been a bustle of energy at the cave's mouth with last-minute preparations and a song of farewell from those remaining. But that was all behind us. We were now on an expedition into the unknown.

On our backs, we carried crude, skin knapsacks tied around our shoulders with handmade rope. We had enough rabbit jerky to last a few days, several blades and the quartz nodules or cores to detach more, and extra spears—both non-tipped and hafted with stone points—at my urging.

We would find water along the way.

There had been a lively discussion about our traveling clothes. Wren wanted as few as possible to speed the departure, but Hand and I prevailed in adding a couple of key items to our kits. We each had an extra piece of thick hide for the cold I knew was coming.

I also insisted that we needed shoes. I could see that their feet were toughened from a lifetime of walking barefoot over all sorts of terrain. But they had rarely embarked on such a long trip before.

So I demonstrated how to make a simple foot covering by wrapping a strip of deer hide around the foot and tying it off above the ankle. It was makeshift, but it was better than going shoeless for what I estimated would be a 300-mile journey. At least for me.

We were leaving behind the mild weather of southern Iberia, and as our small band tramped northward, I reached up to feel the ring still hanging from my neck. Carolyn's ring.

I pressed on it for good luck.

We were going to need it.

◆ ◆

On Hand's advice, we had shifted our direction to the northwest and were now slowing as we started to climb into the higher elevations of what I knew was present-day Parque Natural Los Alcornocales. We needed to pass this area—full of deep gorges and high peaks—to get to the gentle plains that stretched northeast from Cadiz to Cordoba.

We moved along footpaths made by animals or people—hopefully by the very people we were following—through the groves of cork oak trees, but as the elevation rose, the paths disappeared.

At the same time, I watched my Neanders struggle to keep up the four-mile-per-hour pace we had started with. They wanted to take breaks when I wanted to keep going. At first, I couldn't understand why.

Our ability to communicate had improved by learning more of each other's spoken words and by understanding the meaning of our body language. But my asking why they took so many breaks yielded no clear answers beyond what I had learned in my research and could see with my own eyes.

Neanderthals had a different body anatomy. Besides being smaller and more heavily built, they had shorter lower legs and forearms. There was scientific debate about whether their hip joints were different, and if their ability to engage in long endurance activities was limited compared to us modern Sapiens.

But whatever the reasons, I welcomed the descent to the Cadiz plain and the pick-up in walking speed. The psychology of going downhill seemed to override any anatomical shortcomings.

We were midway through our second day when we came to a fast-flowing stream roaring through a narrow ravine. Although this was supposed to be a drier part of Spain—at least in the present-day—rainfall usually picked up starting in October. It had drizzled all night and morning, and the torrent we now faced was flush with muddy water.

I watched the group get agitated. They started pacing back and forth along the riverbank, shouting at the water.

Confused, I quickly found a wide turn in the stream with a quieter pool that would be easy to swim across. As I started to get in to test its depth, Wren's strong grip on my arm pulled me back.

"*Udo*," he said, pointing at the water and shaking his head.

I knew *Udo* meant water, and I repeated it and raised my shoulders and hands in question.

He was adamant and shook his head again. He wasn't going in. And from their frightened faces, neither were the others. Then I realized why.

I had once offered to teach a friend how to improve his swimming. He was a bodybuilder, whose thick, short body bulged with muscles. Like these Neanders.

And when I tested my friend's ability to float in the deep end of the pool, he sank like a stone. The density of his body—muscle weighs more than fat—wouldn't allow him to stay on top of the water without great effort.

So my Neanders were sinkers and couldn't swim! But we needed to get to the other side of the stream.

After a quick search, I found a shallow spot that was

only waist deep. Standing in the middle of the water and bracing against the strong current, I helped each from the group over. They were clearly terrified, but I managed to get them across safely.

"Udo," I said afterward, pointing at the water and moving my head up and down. "Good Udo."

But they all shook their heads together. No.

◆ ◆

On the seventh day, we found a clue. It was a shell necklace similar to the one Brassy wore. Wren held it up for us to see.

"Tepa!" he announced, gripping the necklace and shaking it. This was the name he used for his wife and mother of his daughter, Tepela. No nicknames needed for these two.

We were on the right track.

We had just passed to the north of the Sierra de Gredos mountains, roughly in line with present-day Madrid. This was the high plateau of the steppe-tundra of northern Spain. A landscape very different from the one we had left. A vast, treeless plain of grasses and shrubs bending to a relentless wind. And it was bitterly cold.

The Neanders seemed less affected by the cold than me, most likely because of their shorter body structure. But they were not immune to it. Movement generated heat, and we kept up a pace—if somewhat slower—to stay in constant motion.

Wrapped in every bit of covering we possessed, we followed a faint trail through the landscape where the only thing we heard was the sound of the wind blowing through the brush.

We trekked into the night and were preparing to stop and start a fire when Shorty lifted his head and sniffed. Soon, I could smell it, too. Cooking.

Slowly making our way around a slight rise in the land, we halted as soon as we saw it. A fire. With people around it.

We immediately crouched down and started crawling forward on the hard ground. We came to a clump of grass and hid behind it, watching.

A group of five men stood around the fire. They were lean, and I could see by the firelight that they had dark skin. They were Sapiens.

And huddled together next to the fire were a Neanderthal woman and a young girl.

Tepa and Tepela.

Wren started to release a high-pitched howl but Hand and Shorty piled on top of him and put hands over his mouth to silence him.

He struggled at first but then lay still and nodded his head, acknowledging the situation.

Rolling on his back, his breath coming out in clouds, Wren fixed me with a cold stare and tapped himself on the chest with a closed hand.

"Rr-in," he said quietly, still tapping. He meant

himself. Wren.

Then he pointed at me with the same hand.

"Tum kuk," he said.

He gestured again and repeated my name.

Then he put his index finger on the ground and started making circles with it.

He looked up at me and the others joined him. All three tilted their heads at the same time.

They wanted to know what the next part of my plan was.

16

A veil of clouds over a thin crescent of moon provided the perfect cover.

The Sapiens had posted a single guard while the others slept. And my three companions had quietly moved and positioned themselves to different spots around the smoldering fire, staying well out of sight.

I waited with Wren, the tallest of them, and finally nudged him on the back to start the operation.

Wren began to wail in a haunting, rising-and-falling voice that was picked up by the other two out in the darkness. The singing ebbed and flowed in an eerie chorus that quickly caught the attention of the guard. He stood, his spear outstretched, turning in all directions.

Soon, he was joined by the other men, who were

clearly shaken and frightened by the unusual sounds surrounding them.

I had guessed that odd noises in the middle of the night would trigger irrational and primitive beliefs in these ancient men. And it was working.

The Sapiens, speaking rapidly in an unfamiliar language, were becoming unnerved and now running into each other with increasing panic. And it didn't help when their captives added their singing to the wailing noises.

We were ready for the next phase.

I climbed atop Wren's shoulders, and we wrapped extra skins around us as a disguise.

When Wren stood, I looked down from my high spot and was satisfied. We would appear as a single, towering creature, and if the unnatural wailing hadn't fully frightened these men, the sight of a tall monster surely would.

As our tandem beast approached the low fire, I started adding my own vocalizations, thinking back to all the horror movies I'd seen in my life.

Undulating and ghostly sounds now encircled the Sapiens, who were becoming distraught with confusion and fear.

As soon as Wren and I came into the light of the fire, the Sapiens screamed and fled into the night in different directions. All except for one.

The lone Sapien grabbed hold of Tepa and held her tightly in front of him, a blade to her throat. He hurled angry words at us as we walked closer, and I could sense that Wren was losing his self-control.

With the flash of an idea, I kicked Wren and leaned aggressively forward. We started to tip and I was soon pitching toward the hostage holder.

At the same moment, Hand appeared out of the darkness running full speed at the Sapien.

Hearing Hand's footsteps, the man turned but suddenly stumbled, pulling Tepa to the ground with him. She tried to cry out but her throat was cut, blood spurting.

The man was momentarily shocked by his blunder but quickly jumped to his feet to meet Hand's advance with the blade and his fists.

As the two met and fought, I regained my footing and instinctively rushed at them with my own blade extended.

Hand and the man were clinched and spinning together like two fighting beetles, and when the Sapien's back presented itself to me, I didn't hesitate.

I plunged the stone blade deep into the man's back. Then I stabbed him twice more before he slid down, limp and lifeless.

I looked into the wide-open eyes of Hand while I heard Wren sobbing over Tepa behind me. Turning, I could see that she wouldn't survive.

What had I done? Two humans of different species lay dead, both—one way or another—because of me.

I had taken an active role in the past. I had witnessed

extreme violence but also initiated it. What future events would cascade from this night?

Again I thought: What had I done?

◆ ◆

We wasted no time retracing our route south. We didn't see the Sapiens again but were taking no chances with them coming after us. We pushed the pace as hard as we could and well past nightfall each day.

We took turns carrying Tepa's body, bundled tightly in skins, over our shoulders. Once inside the pine forests of central Spain, we crafted a crude travois drag from two sapling poles and a mesh of thin boughs to hold her.

Tepela alternately walked alongside us or rode on our backs. She seemed mature for her age—I guessed four or five—and she appeared to take in her mother's death without emotion. But she clearly wanted to get back home, a feeling shared equally by all of us.

I spent each day thinking about my future. There wasn't much else to do except walk, eat, sleep, and worry.

As much as I was getting used to my new situation, the yearning to get back to my time was strong.

Some of it was selfish and even superficial. Visions of a hot shower and a soft bed crowded my daydreams along with fantasies of quitting my job and promoting my experiences to fame and fortune. But other emotions gnawed at my gut.

I felt the loss of Carolyn deeply. And I needed some sort of closure with her and the baby, Devin. I felt in my heart that both of them were gone, but I had to know it for a fact.

And seeing Wren holding and playing with Tepela only left me with a profound emptiness and a reminder of what I was missing.

I hoped the self-centered thoughts—personal loss, money, fame—weren't eclipsing the bigger picture of this adventure. And the important question: Was I changing the future with my actions here in the past? And were those changes beneficial overall or not? And for whom?

Then I had a wild thought. What if I was altering the past so I never have that shitty childhood? And Carolyn never gets on that boat?

Then the thinking explodes. What if I was creating a future where Carolyn is never born? Or—gulp—I'm never born. Holy crap.

And I was only thinking about myself and those closest to me. What about others?

What about my Neanderthals? Could I help by giving them an edge over their Sapien rivals? As crazy as it sounded, could I even help to save them? Or delay their demise? And what would that ultimately mean to my world in 2019?

As I drifted off to sleep each night, I wondered if I'd been given the rare opportunity to change the arc of human history. To make the world a better place, as clichéd as that sounded. Or maybe the opposite.

There were so many what-ifs.

By the time we reached the start of the peninsula, I could make out the black raptors soaring around the peak of the Rock of Gibraltar and hear their far-off, screeching calls.

I was close to having my mind made up.

◆ ◆

The whole band greeted us at the cave entrance with a full range of emotions. Passionate hugs of joy mixed with tearful wailing at the sight of Tepa's body.

As the four of us devoured a meal of tortoise, mussels, and pine nuts around the fire, questions were answered, and stories of our adventure told and retold many times.

The weather had shifted in the two weeks we were gone. Temperatures were dropping and the winter rains had started. It wasn't a big change—the seasonal shifts here were mild—but as I curled up in my sleeping fur, listening to the rainfall outside the cave, the group singing started and I kept thinking about those Sapiens we had encountered.

How many more were living to the north? Were some tracking us? How long would it take them to arrive here at Meredith's Cave? And what would happen then?

I fell asleep with my bubbling, troubling thoughts.

And awoke to gentle prodding by Grandpa.

"Puk," he insisted with his voice and body language. Come.

Once I stood I saw the reason.

The entire group had gathered around Tepa, who was wrapped in more skins and adorned with several necklaces made of feathers and shells.

Chanting in uncharacteristically low, mournful voices, Wren and three others picked up the body, and everyone started a slow procession toward a spot on the south wall I hadn't noticed before. It was on the opposite side of the sleeping area from the art gallery. There was a narrow opening that had been completely sealed with large stones.

Two men were removing the stones one by one while the rest of us joined in the chanting and then started a slow, shuffling dance, swaying our bodies in the same spot from side to side.

Suddenly, everyone stopped.

Grandpa held up a special feather he had taken from a type of altar near the main fire, approached Tepa's body, and ceremoniously wove the feather through her hair. He said what must have been a short prayer, and then the swaying and chanting restarted.

Once the opening was cleared enough for us to enter, we filed into a crooked passageway with two torches lighting our way.

We finally entered a small chamber with indentations or pockets dug out of the rock face. And each cavity contained a body—or a skeleton—bent into a fetal position. Which explained the strong tang of decomposing flesh.

This was a burial chamber, sealed off to protect the corpses from scavengers. And us from the smell.

The chanting and dancing continued while Wren placed and positioned Tepa's body in one of the open spaces. Murmuring his own private words, he then placed a beautifully carved flint handaxe on top of her body. He took a step back as the chanting rose in volume to fill the chamber.

I'd been to several funeral services, but none could match the soul-stirring poignancy—and other-worldness—of this one.

After the burial was concluded and we were back in the main chamber, I sought out Brassy and Rabbit. I finally found them sitting together near the cave entrance watching the rain come down and puddle into small pools. A bright mist covered the plain beyond the cave.

I sat down next to Rabbit and he immediately hugged my legs. I patted his shaggy-haired head and looked at Brassy. She smiled warmly and nodded as she watched us. She had a glow in her blue eyes that lit up her whole face.

She moved closer and circled an arm around mine. I smelled the distinctive odor that was characteristic of the women here. Something like eucalyptus. Maybe to ward off bugs. It wasn't unpleasant.

Then she reached up with her other hand and placed it on top of the ring I still wore under my skin mantle.

"Rrring," she said tentatively. There was a subdued gentleness to the sound that contradicted her brassy voice and hard demeanor. Like there was a different person hiding under the coarse exterior.

"Yes," I said, placing my hand over hers.

She sighed and rested her head against my shoulder.

I closed my eyes and listened to the rain.

I felt a strengthening connection with these two along with an inner struggle. As much as I wanted to help these people and their future, *my* future was in going back to 2019. My life was there.

I had to return to the lake.

17

This time I did it right.

I surfaced and immediately knew I was back. And, surprisingly, with no time having passed at all. It was still night and there was Santiago in his little skiff, shaking his head. The police boat had just come to a stop, its wake rocking me.

"I thought I told you to stay away!" the same officer shouted at me. He muttered something under his breath. "Let's bring him in."

As we motored back to the harbor, with Santiago trailing us and me wrapped in another blanket—no one seemed to notice that I had no diving gear and wore only my shorts—I tried to process what was happening.

I had intentionally left all my modern equipment

behind so I could focus on the ring and thong around my neck with their totemic, time-traveling properties. And it had worked. I was back in 2019. I only hoped it was the *same* 2019, or close to it.

But to my prehistoric senses, things felt—even smelled—different. The air was heavy, the odor of fuel oil unmistakable. And most of all, the sounds. Motors whining, buoys clanging.

There were sounds in the past I had just left, but they were subtle. Birds calling, winter frogs croaking, wind whistling. I had re-entered the cacophony of the modern world.

I spent the night in the same police station, but this time in a cell. Alone.

"For your protection," the guard said.

My protection?

There had been more violence. Another boat bombing during the night. Aimed at the same company that owned Carolyn's boat. And more pub fights. I heard all about it from the cells around me. Everyone seemed driven to speak, and at full volume.

There was no hypnotic chanting or communal singing while I sat on a hard bench, hands pressed against my ears. I was hoping for some peace and quiet so I could sleep. It never came.

Victoria bailed me out the next morning with a set of clothes and a promise that I would appear in the Magistrate's Court in a week to explain my misdeeds. We walked to the same restaurant.

"Why'd you do it?" she asked after ordering two coffees. "Why did you defy the police and put yourself at risk again?"

Lining up the silverware, I was still trying to grasp what had happened to me. Was it all just a dream, or had I really been transported to and from 40 kya?

I touched the bag that was clamped between my legs on the chair. No. It was real. It had happened.

I smelled the sublime aroma of the coffee and stared at the smooth Formica surface of the table.

What was I going to tell her? That I'd just spent more than three weeks in the company of her precious fossils? That I knew for a fact that Neanderthals had an upright posture, created art, buried their dead, and sang to each other every night?

That they were much closer to modern humans than anyone in this world thought?

I put down the coffee, pulled a long breath through my nose, and made the decision. I just couldn't keep it bottled up inside. What if something happened to me and my discovery went unrevealed?

So I told her.

As I gave her the short version of my time in the past, I watched her eyes widen and her jaw slowly fall. She was riveted in place, unable to speak, which was not her normal state.

When I was done, I took a final sip of coffee, now cold, and waited.

She blinked several times in a row.

"Either you're mad, or you've just changed both of our lives in a very big way."

"I'm not mad or insane. It happened. Here."

I pushed one of Brassy's pierced shells across the table.

"It can't be," she whispered, staring but too afraid to touch it.

"It is. Proof of Neanderthals' portable, decorative art from at least 40,000 years ago."

I tapped my finger next to the small shell. "Take it and date it. You'll see."

She narrowed her eyes. "You could have taken this from the dig."

I laughed. "And you know there's no evidence of jewelry or symbolic body decoration relating to Neanderthals from any site on the Iberian Peninsula. Including yours in Meredith's Cave. Right?"

"Right," she murmured, but—I could tell—still suspicious.

And I was ready.

"I knew you'd want more proof."

I sent my *pièce de résistance* across the table: the tip from the blackened stick Grandpa had used on the large painting. It had bits of colored pigment clearly showing.

"This will be easy to carbon date," I said. "It's a tool for painting."

Her face telegraphed confusion. "But there aren't any paintings in the cave."

I leaned over the table and made a drawing motion with my index finger.

"No paintings that you've discovered. Yet." I grinned. "Trust me, they're there."

Victoria stared at me and then at the two objects in front of her. I watched her twist her lips in concentration while she grabbed her unused table napkin and carefully bundled up the shell and the painting tip in it. Then she reached across the table and put her hand on mine.

"Assuming you're not lying and making all this up . . . and assuming, just for argument's sake, this loony tale of yours is true—and I'll need the dating results first—then we can go to the next step."

"Which is?" I said, wanting to hear her next move.

"Which is, that we'll need a plan. A careful plan. Do you go back for more evidence? Do I come with you? What tools or recording devices do we need?"

I noticed how quickly she had inserted herself into my story. She was, of course, thinking about her career and what this would do for it. Her stardom would increase a thousandfold. She would be launched into the scientific stratosphere.

And I would rise with her. Not on the same path, but the consequences for me could be enormous. No more career blunders, no more second-rate articles. Hell, I could tour the world just giving speeches. My bad luck would finally change.

But I wasn't sure I trusted Victoria. While I needed

her credibility, her ambitions were legendary. She was cut-throat.

Had I made a mistake telling her?

◆ ◆

I gave myself two days to take care of business and ponder my next steps.

At the top of the list was Carolyn. I read online that her body, along with three others, had not been found after a day of searching. While not officially declared dead—it was too soon for that—I knew deep down that I had lost her and our unborn baby.

I sat on the bed in my hotel room and sobbed and ached that first night. I felt hollowed out with grief and sadness. They were my family. My first real family.

Not sure what to do next, I checked the Violence Tracker site on my laptop. Angered by the pointless violence of the boat bombing, I'd stumbled on this site that used statistics and charts to show how everything from terrorist attacks to gun homicide rates had been steadily ticking upward.

Except the red violence trend line that glowed on the graph in front of me now angled *down*. The world was getting *less* cruel and violent overall. The opposite of what I expected.

I dug a little deeper on the internet.

I read that World War II had ended in early March 1945. But how could that be when Germany didn't surrender until May of that year?

Then I read that the infamous concentration camps had been liberated much earlier than I remembered. Buchenwald, Bergen-Belsen, Mauthausen . . . all freed by the Allies sooner than the history I knew. Or thought I knew. Which meant that thousands—no, tens of thousands—of lives had been saved.

What?

I moved to a more recent event: the September 11 attacks of 2001. I'd watched on TV as the second plane hit the World Trade Center. Then later learned how the plane heading to the U.S. Capitol—United Flight 93—had crashed near Shanksville, Pennsylvania, after a struggle between the hijackers and the passengers.

But now, sitting at the small desk in my hotel room, the laptop screen told a different story. Wikipedia stated that the passengers had actually regained control of the plane and had managed to land it safely at a nearby airport. Forty-four lives were saved.

I couldn't believe what I was reading. So I read it again. And again. Then I went to more history sites and they all told the same story. Flight 93 had not crashed. At least not in the world I had re-entered.

Which could mean only one of two things. Either I had entered a different timestream with a different present, or I was still on the same space-time continuum, but with an altered timeline.

I couldn't help but link all this with the gentle warm-heartedness exhibited by my Neanderthals. For sure, they weren't loveable Ghandis, but their overall philosophy was one of unity and harmony.

What if this different world had already evolved with more of their spirit? And what if I had been the cause of that?

In other words, what if I had already changed things?

But there was an inconsistency. A contradiction.

It seemed that anything I was personally connected with in this present—the boat bombings, the pub violence—had not moved toward harmony and peacefulness. Just the opposite. More conflict. More cruelty. More brutality.

How could this be?

I had no explanation other than that anything relating directly to me and my personal involvement was in a kind of cocoon. A sphere or a web that could not be altered. But anything else was fair game.

It was a hazy theory, but it was all I had.

In any case, the butterfly effect was real. I had influenced the present—some present—with my actions in the past. Not enough to erase Carolyn's getting on that boat. But enough to affect global history.

I had done *something*. I was a butterfly beating its wings.

The implications of this were breathtaking. If I had affected history after only one short visit to the past, what would happen if I did it again?

What if I stayed longer? What if I took an even more active role? What if...

My mind started spinning along with the ceiling fan above me. I had to stop thinking. Had to get out of the hotel and breathe some fresh air.

18

After walking the narrow streets and lanes of Gibraltar for about an hour to clear my head, I went into an art store. It was a tiny place filled with craft supplies, and tucked in the corner was exactly what I needed: a small, blank journal with acid-free Arches pages.

Which meant the paper, if stored correctly, would last for hundreds, if not thousands, of years. I could make ink from charcoal and water. And for writing, a quill from a bird's feather wouldn't be hard to fashion. I would have a way to record my journey when I went back.

If I went back.

Was I deciding?

I had already ruled out taking a camera back. Photoshop for stills and "deep fakes" for video—there was too much potential criticism of manipulated images and "fake news." I was a competent photographer who knew well how to falsify camera imagery. No one would believe that I had photographed living Neanderthals.

Best not to open that can of worms. Just stick to old-fashioned analog tools that could be decisively dated.

Passing by the Gibraltar Natural History Museum, I popped in and found another thing I was looking for. In a display of prehistoric artifacts was an *atlatl*.

Supposedly invented by *H. sapiens*, these spear-throwers were simple wooden sticks that used leverage to increase the velocity—and distance—of a small spear or dart. Basically, it was a straight or slightly bent shaft and a spur at one end to hold the spear.

I made a quick sketch of it in the journal. Just in case.

Walking along Main Street with my new supplies, the afternoon sun slanting in warm and golden, I next called my editor, Ron, in New York.

"Tom, where's my content?" he asked. "Where's the story?"

"Forget that story," I said.

"What do you mean forget it? You're on assignment, remember?"

I ignored his question. "Do you want the story of a lifetime? Something that will put your crappy rag in front of the whole world, scientific and otherwise?"

"What are you talking about? You're—"

"I said, do you?"

"What—"

"You'll get what I've got, when I've got it." And I hung up.

Three chores done in a two-hour break was all I needed to make up my mind. I had decided to go back.

I wasn't sure if the motivation was pure self-interest or something greater than my personal ambitions, like changing the past in a more significant way. But there was more to do in 40 kya. And without Victoria or anyone else.

I would do this by myself.

I punched in Santiago's number.

◆ ◆

We motored in the fading light in silence, Santiago scanning around the boat for trouble.

I needed alone-time to think. To confirm my decision again. And to try to understand how I was able to affect the future.

I had proven to myself that I could change the present by altering the past. But only up to a point. Apparently, I couldn't change *my* present. I felt that I was the same *me* in both 40 kya and 2019. And I could move objects between both times. But I had no leg wound in 2019 because I wasn't wounded *then*.

And Carolyn was still missing, presumed dead. I hadn't changed that.

The bubble of me and my existence seemed to stay the same within the time period I was in. Maybe it was a function of randomness or statistics. That with almost eight billion people on the planet, the chance of changing my own history was just too remote?

I had considered the other option, too. That I had moved from one timestream to another. Where one branched off to a Present A while another yielded a Present B. Two different space-time continuums, and I was able to slip between them.

But this was too much to take in. Whatever the truth was, the paradoxes and frustrations of understanding time travel seemed endless. And, honestly, I wasn't that interested in trying to figure them out.

All I knew was that I had traveled to the past and in doing that, had changed the present. This present.

So I stopped trying to comprehend it and focused on what I was about to do next.

It was now dark and Santiago broke the silence.

"No mask? No fins? No wetsuit?"

"No. No need."

I was taking no new gear. Only my journal protected in a Ziplock bag and tucked in the same shorts. Add the plastic bag to the other modern anachronisms that would hopefully disintegrate over time.

I could just make out the puzzled look on the Spaniard's face when the engine quit and the boat came to a stop. We had arrived.

After wordlessly shaking Santiago's hand, I jumped

into the black water feet first.

Treading water to slow my breathing from the shock of the cold, I took hold of the diamond ring that dangled from its shoelace thong and gave it a squeeze. This time, I would hold it fast.

I took a final breath and dove down, kicking and pulling myself with one arm into the inky depths.

Then I felt it. The shift in temperature. A rippling of pressure. The groaning sensation.

It was happening.

If I couldn't change my own history, maybe I would change it for everyone else.

My new butterfly moment had arrived.

PART THREE

The Return

19

Victoria drummed her fingers on the restaurant table. They were supposed to meet to go over details about the trip, and he was late.

She ordered another Coke. She needed her energy up.

She had started off thinking that what Tom was saying was, of course, preposterous. Traveling back in time to be with Neanderthals? A nutty delusion. Idiotic.

But she had never known Tom to make things up or to deal in fantasy. If anything, he was too realistic. Too methodical. Too compulsive. Even fearless once he'd made up his mind.

It just wasn't like him to fabricate a chimera like this.

If he believed it, she would at least have to consider it. Or until she had the dating results from the two artifacts back. And that would take a couple more days.

And as she warmed up to the idea, she couldn't help daydreaming about what, if it were true, this could do for her career. Tenure and a full professorship at a minimum.

Playfully, she mentally outlined the research paper and the potential list of academic journals for it. They would all be clamoring to publish it once the word got out that, not only did she have new evidence about Homo neanderthalensis, *but . . . she had actually visited them!*

Just the thought of it was staggering. She saw herself on the cover of Time. *Maybe even an HBO special.*

No harm in dreaming, right?

The Coke arrived and she downed it in three gulps and started drumming again.

Where is he?

She was starting to get that bad feeling whenever Tom was involved. He had wrecked things before. He could do it again.

Victoria paid her bill and took the stairs to Tom's room and rapped on the door. No answer. Hmm.

Standing at the door and burping from the Coke, she reconstructed their conversation over lunch the day before.

She needed to find the guy with the boat. Santiago.

20

I crawled out of the lake, shook the water off my hands, and pulled out the journal.

After carefully unzipping the plastic bag, I flipped through the book's pages to check. All dry and undamaged. Good.

I stood and turned in a circle. Everything looked the same, but how would I know if I missed the time destination by 1,000 years or so? I hoped the ring was my thread back to the same point in the timeline. I'd know soon enough.

A dark storm mass was building to the north, and the wind was picking up. With nothing on but my cotton shorts, I started moving.

The empty landscape, the bracing air, and the

coming storm brought a surge of energy that coursed through my body. I felt alive with purpose.

I was less than halfway up the long slope to the cave when I heard something. It sounded like mewing. An animal of some type, and by its high-pitched yips, a young one.

Walking slowly in a crouch, I rounded a short hill and stopped. Lying just outside the opening of a burrow was a black hyena cub on its side, twitching. It looked just like a cute, little puppy dog. But I knew better.

Worried that its parents were nearby, I waited a good while and then approached the animal as quietly as I could, picking up a thick stick to use as a weapon. Even though I'd be no match for one or two adult hyenas. They could tear apart an adversary or their prey in a matter of minutes. And leave no trace behind.

I had done a story about hyenas for *Science Alive*, and I'd visited the zoo to study them. And now I smelled the distinctive, foul odor that hyenas deposited from their anal glands to mark and patrol their territories. And I touched the scar on my lower leg to remind me of the danger I was in.

But this cub appeared to be abandoned. And looking more closely, I could see why. The cub was extremely malnourished. Its ribs were showing, rising and falling with each breath.

I had learned that two pups are typically born in a hyena litter and immediately start to fight for dominance.

The stronger cub prevents the other from nursing, leaving it alone after the family moves on without it.

When the cub saw me, it tried to raise its head but couldn't. It was doomed. And that triggered something in me.

In no time, I was holding the weak animal in my arms and continuing on my path up to the caves.

I knew someone who would appreciate having a young pet—even a hyena—to raise.

◆ ◆

As I approached the cave, I spotted two members of my Neanderthal group walking to the communal poop site a couple of hundred feet from the entrance. They looked exactly the same.

I'd done it. Retraced my way to the same time and place. The final verification would come when I saw Rabbit. He was a five-year-old boy, and any change in time would be readily apparent.

Soon, thick, roiling storm clouds joined with a fierce wind to drive everyone, including me, into the cave.

Once safely inside, I took stock of the situation while I listened to the howling wind and walked back toward the main fire with the hyena.

Honestly, I was expecting more of a reception. Even though I felt like I'd been gone for days, apparently no one else did. Then I realized that just as there'd been no gap in time when I traveled ahead to 2019, it was likely identical going the other way. The Neanderthal world I'd left showed all the signs of being the same on re-entry.

Only now I was carrying a hyena cub in my arms and the reactions came swiftly. Each person I encountered turned terrified when they spotted the cub before fleeing into the interior of the cave.

Except for Wren, who confronted me halfway to the fire, standing well back and pointing.

"What is?" he asked in his lower voice, the one he used when he was worried. His language skills had improved considerably because of our regular classes. The sound of his speech was still odd, like the chattering of a parrot trying to mimic a human's voice, but it was becoming easier to communicate with him.

He wasn't asking *what* the cub was. He knew that all too well. He was really asking me *why*.

But he was also used to my unconventional ideas—to them—so he just shook his head.

From my reading, I'd learned that hyenas were not only competitors for food—primarily ones that ran on four legs—but they were also key predators. Even of humans.

Sapien folklore and myths were full of stories of hyenas preying on people, mainly the young and the weak. With their massive, wolf-like builds and the unbelievable power of their bone-crushing jaws and teeth, hyenas were smart and formidable enemies, especially in packs.

Luckily, this little hyena cub that had fallen asleep in my arms was frail and alone. Completely at our mercy. And I was developing an idea that was still a vapor in my mind, but one that could have a significant impact on the Neanders, who I'd noticed had no dogs. But I had to get them to accept this cub first.

"Hyena," I said to Wren, repeating the word slowly and breaking it into its three syllables.

Wren tried but was incapable of producing a similar sound. Instead, he said what I assumed was their word for it: *"Kauta."*

"Kauta," I repeated. I would use their word.

Wren probably knew I had a plan for this hyena cub so he walked with me past the fire to where Brassy and Rabbit sat, both busy chewing on lengths of deer hide, a process that made them soft and supple, like the finest chamois leather.

I quickly verified that Rabbit was still the same lively, long-haired, five-year-old boy I remembered.

Brassy jumped to her feet as soon as she saw the cub, pointing and shouting at it. She wanted no part of this dangerous animal.

Rabbit had a different reaction. Half-squealing with excitement, he ran to me and threw his arms around my legs in what had become a greeting ritual between us.

When I bent down to show him the cub, the boy seemed unsure. But then a big smile spread across his face while he reached out and put a small hand on the cub's head, gently stroking it.

"Kauta," he said.

I stooped and placed the still-sleeping cub on the ground. Rabbit quickly joined it there, petting the animal's soft fur and murmuring quietly in its ear.

Rabbit, whose normal hyperactive personality had just changed to one of restful calm, now had a pet. And so did the rest of the group.

21

Once I'd re-established my connections and settled back into my prehistoric life, it was time to organize the journal and start writing in it. I was going to document everything.

But first, I needed a quill pen and some bona fide Paleolithic ink.

Finding a feather was easy. Feathers were everywhere. They were worn in their hair and attached to necklaces. They were used to swat away flies and, tied together, handled like a broom to clean.

Because these people both hunted and ate birds, there were piles of feathers along the cave's northern wall, and after asking, I was allowed to take whatever I wanted.

The one exception was the feather of the Golden

Eagle, which held a high, symbolic position for these Neanders. The eagles were never hunted for food, but their remains were sometimes found on the savannah. Grandpa wore one eagle feather in his hair, and many more were displayed on the altar that stood next to the fire.

I found a likely quill candidate in a foot-long vulture feather and set about turning it into a writing pen.

I sat outside the cave entrance under a brilliant blue sky left behind by the passing storm front and could feel the coolness of the advancing winter. I started by stripping off the bottom vanes of the feather along with the fluffy afterfeather parts. This gave me a clean shaft to hold in my hand.

Then I had to carefully cut the end into a workable nib. This I did with the same small blade Wren had gifted me after our rescue mission north. Made of quartz, the blade was dangerously sharp, and I concentrated on not slicing up my fingers.

It took me less than an hour to make a simple angle cut of the shaft, trim the end flat, and cut a slit down the middle that would allow the ink to run onto the paper.

With the feather pen made, I moved on to the ink.

It felt like I was on a scavenger hunt, and I noticed I was picking up curious onlookers along the way. They kept their distance but weren't hesitant in making comments and laughing at the antics of their crazy visitor.

Back inside the cave, I collected bits of charred

wood and soot from the fire in a small pouch. Then, with a melon gourd I was given by Brassy, I scooped some stream water from the large central gourd that was always kept full by the younger children.

Retreating to a favorite corner of the cave closer to the entrance, I sat and pulverized the charred wood with a smooth stone and added small amounts of water as I did. As a last step, I strained the ink through a discarded piece of plant-fiber mesh they used for cleaning dirty water.

I ended up with a soupy concoction that was more brown than black and that smelled like a tilled-up garden bed after a long rain.

Satisfied with my handiwork, I gathered my journal and tools and walked down the slope a short distance. I wanted a long view of the cave entrance and the cliff it was part of. I would start with a simple description of my new home in 40 kya.

But now I had an audience. Several of the Neanders had followed me and formed a loose circle waiting to see what I would do next. They were soon joined by Brassy and Rabbit carrying the hyena cub. They, too, were doubtlessly wondering what all the unusual activity was about.

Sitting on a low, flat-topped boulder I opened the journal to its first blank sheet. I dipped the point of the quill into the gourd of ink and wrote with the steadiest hand I could the title of my document in large letters at the top of the page: *My Neanderthals*.

I think I was as amazed as they were by what appeared on the paper. Just two words in dark ink. But such momentous words.

I was now the world's first Paleolithic writer.

◆ ◆

Because I'd attracted an audience, I decided to try an experiment. I was intending to sketch the cave with the new quill to illustrate my words. But when I saw the curiosity in Brassy's eyes, I shifted gears.

I wasn't that proficient in drawing faces, but I could do an okay job. And I wanted to test something I had read.

After asking Brassy to sit in front of me, I started sketching her face on a new blank page. It was evident she didn't understand what I was doing so I kept having to catch her attention in order to capture her likeness.

I started with her large, alert eyes and gradually filled in the heavy brows, wide nose, and downturned mouth, which sometimes switched to an enigmatic Mona Lisa smile that was half smirk, half challenge.

I finished with the unruly auburn hair that pushed out in different directions.

After adding some touches of shadow and texture, I motioned for Brassy to sit next to me on the flat boulder. Once she was seated, I held out the open journal with the drawing and waited for her reaction.

And there was none. No recognition that this was her on the page.

So it was true. I had long ago heard that in primitive cultures, people could not *see* or *read* photographs or other types of realistic images beyond stick or simple figures, like those in the cave. The conventions of visual representation were not there. Even some modern people with a neurological disorder called Prosopagnosia are unable to recognize faces, including their own.

After seeing her bafflement, I stood and walked past the others, showing the sketch to each one of them. All gave me back the same blank stare as Brassy. Except for Rabbit.

When the boy saw the journal page he started laughing and reached out to it. He wanted to touch it, but first, he had to put down the hyena cub that was stretching its legs and making gurgling sounds. The two had clearly bonded.

Seeing an opportunity, I turned to a blank journal sheet and handed the quill to Rabbit and set down the ink gourd next to him.

I showed him how to hold the quill and dip it in the ink, then I guided his hand to the paper and stepped back. I wanted to see what he would do.

I wasn't disappointed.

After getting comfortable holding the feather and making some preliminary spots around the edge of the paper, he settled into a defined rhythm of drawing a series of horizontal lines down the length of the page.

When he reached the bottom, he stopped and looked up at me with wide eyes, wondering what to do.

I turned the paper and touched the next blank sheet.

He immediately started drawing his straight lines again. Not only were the lines level and uniform, but they were also exactly the same length, about two inches. All of them.

After he stopped again at the bottom of the page, I asked for the journal back and stared at the paper in disbelief. Little Rabbit had created a column of perfectly made marks marching down the page as if he were an experienced architectural draughtsman.

I was astonished. This five-year-old Neanderthal boy, who I had suspected of being slightly on the Asperger's spectrum, had just shown me a piece of myself and my own OCD patterns. Me, who loved lining things up in orderly perfection.

What I was seeing in the toothy grin of Rabbit was possibly the beginning of my own twenty-first-century behavior. Some of the DNA sequences in Rabbit, Brassy, and probably many of the archaic hominids who preceded them, were still alive in me.

Science had already proven—in Present Dig Time—that a small amount of ancient Neanderthal DNA was carried by all modern-day *H. sapiens* outside of ancestral sub-Saharan Africa. There was a direct link in the genomes of the two species.

I was looking into the face of my own—and humanity's—past.

22

Weeks went by and we were in the rainy period approaching the winter solstice.

Not that there was a lot of rain, but the skies filled with clouds more often and the nip in the air brought out more skins and thicker hides for covering up. At least, for me. The lower temperatures seemed to have little effect on the Neanders who still seemed comfortable in their near nakedness.

I was now accepted as part of the band and, with my journal always at hand, I observed and documented everything around me. I found the daily activities and roles of my hosts especially interesting, and I was surprised by how blurry the division of labor lines was.

The adult women spent their days gathering edible plants, preparing and cooking food, scraping and working with animal hides, and watching over children. But they were frequently assisted by the men.

Likewise, the women helped the men in the hunting of large prey, especially red deer, horses, and ibex, the wild goat of the area. The men were stronger, but the women were often better at hunt strategy. And the best at butchering the kill on-site. Or so I was told.

The whole communal structure was very egalitarian.

Only the children, who seemed more mature at the same ages than I remembered, were more role defined. When they weren't playing, children were responsible for fetching water from the nearby stream, helping with gathering, and hunting for birds and small mammals, especially mice and rabbits.

They constructed ingenious snares made from honeysuckle vines that they hung or stretched across known animal pathways. The modern theory that Neanderthals were only capable of hunting large, slow-moving animals was clearly wrong.

No doubt because life was hard and perilous, there were few elderly Neanders apart from Grandpa. And he occupied a unique position: storyteller and keeper of oral history, in charge of the wall paintings, and spiritual chief responsible for maintaining the feather altar and leading the main ceremonies and rituals.

But I had the most specialized role of all: teacher from another world.

I convened my language class every evening at the cave's southern wall near the fire. Sometimes the only other students were my regulars: Wren and Brassy, with Rabbit attending when he wasn't playing or trapping. But the result was an overall improvement in our level of communication.

Common words were repeated in both of our tongues, with the exception of certain speech limitations.

Confirming what I had read, they had a hard time forming the *F* and *V* sounds of labiodentals, maybe due to the shape of their heads or the size of their teeth. But our practiced speaking and signing got the important ideas across.

And for some reason, I'd become the final arbitrator of major disputes, which were rare. I was like a traveling circuit judge from the Old West who rode to outlying areas to hold court once a month. A kind of celebrity referee.

And that had happened recently.

The disagreement was between Hand and Shorty and a woman both wanted as a second wife. She sat quietly by the fire with her primary husband, enjoying the argument over her.

Once the two offers and pleadings were finished, everyone turned to me for a resolution. The solution seemed obvious as I walked over to the woman and crouched in front of her.

Turning and pointing to the two men, I said, "Who do *you* want?"

She grinned at me and stood. Then she walked over and put her hand on top of Shorty's head.

"This," she said, smiling. We hadn't covered objective pronouns yet in class.

The entire group started applauding in their unique way: simultaneously slapping both hands rapidly on their chests, which made a deep, muffled sound that reverberated throughout the cave.

We were all so caught up in the spirit of the moment that I didn't sense the change at first. But one look at Wren's face gave it away.

The whole chamber went silent as everyone's eyes focused on the same spot behind me.

I whirled around to see a group of four unfamiliar men standing together just inside the cave entrance, partially blocking its light. And at the front of the group was the scariest man I'd ever seen.

◆ ◆

I'd noticed that my OCD behaviors had lessened around the Neanders. There wasn't as much need for the constant pressing and tapping I did to soothe myself against an unpredictable and hostile world.

But with the sight of these four men at the cave entrance, I instinctively found my thumbnails digging hard into my finger pads.

Their leader exuded an air of menace. His head was shaved except for a scalp lock of dense wiry hair, and the entire head was painted in bold vertical stripes, alternating black and white. Long cactus-like needles pierced his nose and each ear. A thick bear hide hung over his shoulders, complete with dangling paws that reached almost to the ground.

The man looked ready for a fight. And very capable of winning one.

Slowly swinging a massive club, this leader moved his dark brown eyes over us until finally stopping on me. He said something quickly to a man at his side who nodded.

I quickly realized that these two dark men were Sapiens—Minyas—while the other two were clearly Neanderthals. The contrast was easy to see in a mixed group like this. And these Minyas seemed to hold a superior role over the Neanders. How this had come to be was worrying.

After learning that the men were interested in trading, Grandpa, acting as the ceremonial leader, invited them to sit in a special area of the cave near the feather piles.

Several oak logs were arranged in a circle for impromptu meetings like this. Not too far into the cave's interior but close enough to the fire to feel its warmth. A neutral area with enough light to see by.

But even with a plausible reason for the visit, I was nervous and leery of these strangers.

On my group's side of the circle was what I now called the leadership council. Besides Grandpa, there was Wren, the tallest and strongest, Brassy, representing the women, and finally, me, the token Sapien and the outside arbiter.

Gourds of water were handed to the visitors by two small children and the men drank them quickly. Then the formal meeting began.

The sinister-looking leader was talking in a language different from the Neanders but somehow familiar. I had heard it before. Up north.

The man, who had started off speaking to Grandpa, now shifted his attention to me. Maybe he could see that I was also a Sapien and that I held some sort of leadership role.

When I looked at Grandpa, questioning my position in the conversation, he nodded his approval.

After a lot of garbled speech and generous signing, I determined that this group lived two-days walk to the northeast, around present-day Malaga. And they were interested in trading their handaxes for some of the feathers they were studying and that must have held special meaning for them.

Handaxes and feathers were being passed around for inspection when one of the visitors—a young Neanderthal with a long beard—suddenly walked over to Brassy, who sat between me and Wren. He displayed a gruesome smile with missing teeth and reached out to touch one of Brassy's breasts.

She immediately slapped his hand away at the same time that Wren lunged at him, punching him squarely on his broad nose.

The man shouted in pain, fell down, and crawled on

his hands and knees back his spot in the circle.

It occurred to me that these men were interested in more than feathers, and I noticed a twang of jealousy nibbling at me over Brassy. I was becoming protective of her. Or maybe it was more than that.

As hard as it was for me to believe, I couldn't deny a tiny bit of attraction to this Neanderthal woman. I had always gravitated to short women with muscular arms and legs. Carolyn was like that. And so was Brassy.

As the young man tried to reseat himself, their leader savagely struck the side of his face with a fist and pushed him off the log and onto his back.

Now standing, the leader started kicking the man. Hard. It turned into an uncontrollable attack with the downed man curled into a fetal position and grunting with each blow.

I wanted this viciousness to stop so I jumped to my feet and tried to restrain the leader. He pushed me back, glaring, and I could see that he was ready to attack me.

Now everyone was on their feet, yelling and screaming.

Things were about to explode when Grandpa stepped into the middle of the ring and held out both arms. Everyone stopped as the old man slowly pointed with his right hand to the cave entrance.

"Go!" he said in English. Then he repeated the word in his own tongue, jabbing with his hand for emphasis. "Go. Now."

The visit was over. There would be no trading.

As the Sapien leader walked past, he paused and looked directly at me. His brows were lowered and his eyes narrowed. He spoke several unintelligible words in a low, threatening voice at the same time he raised a hand and pointed up to the cave's ceiling.

Then I realized he was pointing to the north. He knew what had happened on the high plateau of northern Spain.

We were not done with this Minya.

23

Two days passed and I couldn't stop thinking about what had happened. A couple of things bothered me.

First, the visiting group consisted of both Neanders and Sapiens. And the Sapiens were clearly in charge.

I knew there were other Neanderthal bands in southern Iberia—Grandpa had confirmed that—but I had never heard of or even read about mixed groups like this. It was a sign of Sapien infiltration into Neanderthal territory and social structure.

The second—and related—concern was the connection between this nearby leader and the Sapiens in the north. Sapiens were no longer a remote threat hundreds of miles away. Now they were close.

And I knew how the story of the Neanderthals ultimately ended sometime around 37 kya. It wasn't a good conclusion for them. The peril was real, the history was known.

Or was it?

I had already changed history once. Could I do it again? And I mean *really* do it.

These thoughts swirled in my head as I led the four children on the well-trodden path from the caves across the peninsula to its western slope where the single known stream ran. Collecting water was a job for the young ones who were always accompanied by at least one adult chaperone for protection. I was now respected enough to have that job today.

It had rained during the night so the stream would be full, and we all sang the silly Hickory Dickory Dock rhyming song in English as we marched single file with our empty goat bladders ready for filling. Rabbit walked with the hyena cub on a rope leash, the fast-maturing animal pulling Rabbit this way and that as it cackled and explored each side of the path.

The two were inseparable, and Rabbit had capably taken on the daily job of feeding the cub a mush of pounded meat mixed with water and blood. After several months the cub would be eating solid food, and Rabbit would have his hands full.

My fanciful hope of having these Neanders domesticate a pack of hyenas seemed improbable, but there were anthropological theories that claimed dog domestication was a key to the advancement of *Homo sapiens*. Hyenas weren't dogs but maybe I was witnessing—and encouraging—a different twist on that hypothesis.

We reached the stream at midday with the low winter sun hidden by a blanket of clouds. The storm had moved southeast over Africa and far-off thunder rumbled somewhere above Algeria.

After we'd filled and tied off our bladders, I walked the group along a muddy path to a quiet pool below a small waterfall. Looking down at the footprints the children made on the path, I couldn't help musing if these wouldn't one day be among the fossilized Neanderthal footprints discovered in 2019 to great fanfare. Footprints clearly made by children but with one large print from a taller individual mixed in.

Were we making history on this mundane errand?

Once stopped, I started sketching the boy's and girl's faces in my journal. And I noticed Tepela crouched at the edge of the pool, her hands in the still water and staring down at her reflection.

"Tepela," she said, laughing and pointing. She seemed to have none of the fear of water that I'd witnessed in the adults on our trip north.

I walked over and squatted next to her, looking down at my reflection next to hers.

"Mooka!" she said excitedly when seeing both of us in the water.

Mooka was their word for themselves. Their people. Neanderthals.

I studied the two reflections. Tepela thought we were the same, but I knew better. Or thought I did.

Being honest with myself, were we really that different? Or even more importantly, were we Sapiens somehow better than them?

I wondered.

◆ ◆

My concerns and apprehensions were temporarily wiped clean the next night. It was the winter solstice. And I didn't need a calendar or a news report to tell me that.

The celebrations to mark the start of the astronomical new year had begun earlier in the day, but the culmination was tonight.

The entire Neander band—I counted 11—was in motion around the fire that blazed bright and lit up the cave. Giant silhouettes danced on the rock walls as we—I had joined them—tramped and shuffled on the packed dirt to the rhythm of the chanting voices.

It was like an ethereal Gregorian chant but much livelier and rowdier. It had the feeling of a New Age mantra-spouting circle. Or even the repetitive beat of a hip-hop rapper.

And the festive atmosphere was amplified by the gourds full of homemade brew I consumed. The sweet drink they called *neek* was their version of the fermented fruit concoction ubiquitous in prison populations in my time. The dried summer fruit—native figs and grapes—was stored deep in the cave for snacking and for alcohol-making. And it was having its effect: I was drunk.

The smell of neek and perspiration mixing with smoke permeated the cave as we heated up from the dancing and discarded our skin coverings piece by piece. I was soon drenched in sweat and feeling euphoric.

I followed Wren around the circle, trying to mimic his footsteps but finding it difficult to balance in my inebriated state. I stopped and immediately collided with Hand, who was next in line behind me. He jerked up and laughed.

"Tum kuk!" he slurred while he slapped me on the back and leaned against me. "I like you," he garbled.

"And I like you," I said, holding him off. "You're a good man."

"Gud men," he repeated while we restarted the dance, me facing him backward.

He pointed across the fire to Brassy who was leading Rabbit. The hyena cub was running alongside, nipping at both their legs.

"You like?"

After Hand had lost out to Shorty in attracting the other woman's affections as a second wife, he had shifted his focus to Brassy, who was resisting his advances.

Which made Brassy's increased attention toward me awkward. And it hadn't gone unnoticed by the other Neanders, who continually kidded me and her about it. They were almost like immature adolescents about this, whispering and giggling.

It was embarrassing and more than a little confusing to have a Neanderthal woman interested in me. Where could this possibly lead?

Hand suddenly announced, "I pee" and broke off from the dancing circle, heading toward the entrance.

I also had to pee so I followed him out.

We stood next to each other in the dark, stars gleaming between wisps of clouds that covered a rising moon. His stream gushed like a horse compared to mine.

"You go to you?" he said, again standing awkwardly close, as they tended to do.

The meaning was clear. Was I going back to my people? And for me by inference, was I going back to my time? They had never asked before, and I assumed they thought I'd just wandered away from my own band of Sapiens. Or been thrown out. So it was a good question.

Standing next to Hand, shivering from the cool air on my sweaty skin, I had to ask myself.

When *was* I going back?

24

It took a day to sleep off the effects of the solstice celebration. I was still hungover from the neek and a little sore from all the dancing, but I was ready for the hunt. Meat supplies were low, and it was time to secure more. They had a varied diet, but meat was the most prized food source.

It was a mixed group that headed out onto the savannah plain that angled down toward Africa and the line of cairns. Two men, two women. The best hunters and the best butchers. Wren, Shorty, Brassy, and another woman with no nickname yet. And me.

We had left the cave early but now the sun was bright, climbing on its low winter arc in a cloudless sky. It would be a hard day under the sun so our clothing was light: loincloths and thin capes for the men and laced-together tunics—prehistoric dresses—for the women. I had my deteriorating shorts and a skin mantle.

And everyone now wore simple deer hide shoes. I had convinced them. Or maybe they considered the shoes as status symbols. Like Air Jordans, and I was their Michael.

The best I could tell, wild horses were the prey. Horses provided the biggest bang for the energy buck. There were other grazers and browsers too—ibex, deer, boar, and aurochs—but horses were the most valued. Lots of meat with less risk of injury or death.

I was honored to be included. And I was prepared.

I'd spent two days turning my journal sketch of a spear-thrower into reality. Using the small blade I now always carried, I trimmed and turned a four-foot-long oak branch with a bow in it into an atlatl, complete with the spur on the end to hold a fire-hardened spear.

I was hoping the atlatl and four small spears to use with it—each about four feet long—would be enough for the hunt.

Their weapons were heavy, stone-tipped spears and clubs, and they laughed when they saw my hunting tools, but I had been practicing with the spear-thrower and had partially mastered the hinged throwing technique. I wasn't going to make the Olympic javelin team, but I was hoping I wouldn't embarrass myself.

We walked slowly through the plain's grasses and scrub bushes, scanning for movement. Quail, rabbits, and other small animals were ignored. We had one goal.

"*Gagak!*" Wren suddenly said in a quiet but excited voice. Their word for horse.

I looked in the direction he was pointing and there they were. A small herd of about a dozen grazing horses 400 yards away. Dark brown with necks down and tails swishing. They hadn't noticed us yet.

Earlier, Brassy had suggested a circular pincer strategy for surrounding any animals we came upon. So now, at her signal, we crouched low and split apart to start the encircling.

Once we were in position, I could see Brassy through a sparse copse of olive trees, and I saw her nod her head. Time to spring the trap.

Still in a crouch, I started moving toward the horses and saw the others doing the same from their sides of the circle, which was tightening. We were lucky there was no wind to carry our scent, and the horses seemed oblivious to the approaching danger.

I was 20 yards away when one horse abruptly raised its head, ears swiveling back to front. Then it splayed its front legs out to the side. The alert was raised.

Brassy shouted something and everyone rushed in at the horses that were trying to decide which way to bolt. But we were on all sides and closing in fast.

The horses squealed and raced in different directions hoping to fly past us and escape.

I saw Wren throw his heavy spear at a fleeing horse and barely miss, the spear nicking but glancing off its back. Brassy and the other woman had similar close misses.

Shorty tried to thrust his spear into a horse running past him, but the horse suddenly pivoted and almost trampled him. He was able to jump out of the way at the last second, but the horse got away.

That left me, and I was ready. With a horse coming right at me.

I drew back the atlatl and mini spear with my right arm, stepped forward, and launched the projectile with all my strength at the charging horse.

The spear hit the horse's forehead between the eyes with a loud crack. The horse skidded to a stop and reared up on its hind legs, its head gushing blood from where the spear was implanted.

The horse towered over me, its front legs pawing the air wildly. Just when I thought I was going to get crushed by this horse, it fell back on its rump and rolled onto its side. Dead.

Part of me hated killing a horse. To this modern man, horses were beautiful creatures that symbolized freedom and power. But to my Neander band, horses were food. Nothing more. And this horse would provide meat for days to come.

I knew this, but I found it impossible to watch—much less take part in—the butchering of this splendid animal. So I walked away, using my need to pee as the excuse.

I hadn't realized we were this close to the lake that

was the start of my adventure into this world, so I headed toward it, seeing the sun sparkle on its ruffled surface.

Thinking I might take a quick dip to rinse off my sweat and clear my mind in the cold water, I bent over to pull off my clothes when I heard a familiar voice call out my name.

"Tom?"

I jerked up and gasped.

Emerging out of the lake was Victoria.

◆ ◆

I was speechless as I watched Victoria walk toward me, her long red hair slicked back, her mouth pulled up into a gloating grin. She had on a white shirt that was plastered to her body, showing the bikini top and blue-jean shorts she wore underneath.

"You thought you could disappear with *that* secret?" she said when she reached me. "The carbon-dating results backed up your story. No way were you going to bypass me on this."

I finally found my voice. "How'd you do it?"

She smiled. "How do you think? I listened closely to what you said and studied what you gave me. And when you were nowhere to be found, I drew the logical conclusion."

I had underestimated her ambitions.

"And you . . ."

"I hired Santiago. Paid him enough to give me the details. It didn't work at first, but then I figured it out."

She held up her closed hand and opened it. There was Brassy's pierced shell I'd given her at lunch. She'd used that as her totemic link to the past.

Now what was I going to do?

I caught myself pressing my finger pads while I ran through scenarios in my mind. Run away and hope she gets lost? Convince her to go back?

I was stuck and left with only one real option.

"You're here so let's make the best of it. But I have some ground rules."

She tilted her head to me. "Really? Okay, let's hear them."

"First, you need to follow my lead. I know these people better than you."

She laughed. "Oh, so you're the expert now? After what, a few weeks?"

"Well, that's more time than you. This is not a lecture or a lab. Or digging for fossils with a hotel to go to afterward. We're actually here in the past with living, breathing people."

I watched her eyebrows dip and her mouth tighten. But she said nothing.

Then, "Okay, what else?"

"If I say that something is wrong or that we're in danger, it means we are and you follow my instructions. Without question. Agreed?"

She just looked at me. She was not used to being a

follower. And especially not of me.

"Agreed," she finally said. "So what's next?"

A cold wind blew from the north as we made our way back to where the others were. Slowly. On top of shivering, Victoria's bare and civilized feet were no match for the thorn bushes, sharp rocks, and uneven ground of the savannah plain.

And her impossibly white skin—as white as her button-down shirt—would soon succumb to the sun's rays, which were undoubtedly stronger in 40 kya without the greenhouse gases and atmospheric particles of modern times.

Most archeological diggers were well-tanned from being outside, but Victoria spent most of her time underground in caves. I had to get her into the warmth and protection of Meredith's as soon as possible.

We finally arrived at the butchering site and the group's reaction was nothing short of stunned stupefaction. All four faces showed bewilderment at seeing a tall, red-haired, chalk-skinned woman walking toward them.

And Victoria was equally shocked at seeing this group of archaic humans. "Oh, my God," she said repeatedly as she stopped and took in the sight. "It's really true. You did it. We're really here."

She puckered her lips and let out a long breath. "It's ...it's unreal."

Victoria then let out a shriek at the sight of the butchered horse. Only its head remained somewhat intact. Everything else was in a pile of dismembered limbs, large cuts of meat, and internal organs. Surprising to me, the smell wasn't unpleasant. Like blood mixed with good earth for planting.

"We killed a horse," I said unnecessarily.

Victoria started to gag but stopped with Brassy's approach.

Without speaking, the short Neanderthal reached up a blood-covered hand to touch Victoria's red hair. Brassy had reddish-brown hair herself, but this flaming color was in a different category.

Victoria reflexively recoiled and stepped back.

Brassy said something I couldn't understand then looked at me and frowned. "You?" she said, her questioning eyes moving from me to Victoria and back again.

"No," I answered quickly, understanding immediately that she thought Victoria and I were a couple.

Victoria snickered and shook her head. "So, I see you've got a new girlfriend."

I was about to protest when Shorty suddenly stepped to Victoria and smiled up at her.

"Minya," he said, inclining his head toward her.

Then he rapped his closed fist on his chest. He beamed and wagged his finger between the two of them.

"Minya. Me. Wife."

I laughed quietly, but Victoria didn't think it was funny.

25

Back in cave—once I'd straightened out Shorty and Victoria had eaten some dried figs—I took Victoria away from the others to the meeting circle near the feather piles to talk. There was just enough light from the fire so we could see our faces.

I said, "Look, your coming here is making things more complex. I decided to come back alone. I have my reasons for that."

She snorted. "And my reasons don't count? Don't forget, I'm the dig director. You wouldn't have done any of this if it weren't for me. You owe me."

"I *owe* you?"

"You decided to tell me. We were talking about how to get back here and—"

"I never promised that. And you don't understand."

"Don't understand what? It seems obvious to me. We've gone back in time. We—"

"What you don't understand is that your being here changes things."

She studied me for a moment.

"Changes what things?"

"The future. Our present."

"What do you mean?"

I shut my eyes and took a long breath through my nose to relax. "I mean our 2019 will now be even more different."

"*More* different?"

"Yes. Something I didn't tell you at that lunch. I found discrepancies."

"What do you mean: *discrepancies?*"

"Things we knew to be true that no longer are. That can only be attributed to my having traveled here. To this time and place. You know, the butterfly effect."

She was silent and nodded. "Okay. And?"

"And now your being here will definitely change things even more."

"You don't know that. I'm well-versed in Lorenz's butterfly effect—and by the way, he first used a seagull as the example—and an important part of it is unpredictability. It's called "chaos theory" for a reason. Chaos is, by definition, nonlinear. Maybe we'll cancel each other out. One butterfly counteracting the other. Who knows?"

"Who knows? I know what I saw when I went back.

And there's no telling now with you here."

"Well, it's too late. I'm here and I'm going to make the most of this. I don't plan to stay long. Two weeks or so should do it. I want to observe and gather evidence. Then I'll go back."

She stopped and leaned in toward me. "Hopefully, with you."

I watched while Victoria fumbled with her jeans pocket and finally pulled out a small camera. "I brought this along to help."

I immediately recognized it as a waterproof digital Nikon.

I chuckled. "You think I didn't think of that? You're wasting your time with a camera that's going to run out of battery before you know it. I'll let you borrow my journal if you want."

She stared defiantly at me. "I think I'll do both. If that's all right with you," she said in a mocking tone.

I sighed and nodded. "Fine. But please be inconspicuous with the camera. They don't know what it is."

She gave me a triumphant smile. Then she relaxed and let her eyes drift.

"Look around us. We've traveled back in time! It's ... it's incredible. It's—"

She paused, weighing her next words.

"It's much too important to bottle up in one person's insecurities and weird ways."

"What weird ways?" Now I was defensive.

She looked at me with hard eyes.

"You know exactly what I mean. You're a quitter. A self-sabotager. Always were. Remember that final at U.T.?"

How could I forget that screwup?

The final exam for Intro to Anthropology was printed in one of those "blue books" filled with multiple-choice questions and pages for essay answers.

After opening my book, I saw that the margins on the pages weren't uniform. The outside margins were much wider than the inside ones. How could they have printed such a mess?

So I borrowed a pair of scissors from the professor and carefully trimmed down all the outside margins to make them even. To make them just right.

Unfortunately, I spent so much time on the trimming operation that I failed to finish the exam by the deadline. I barely passed the course and eventually dropped out to start working.

But I had changed. I'd learned how to channel my obsessions into positive action. Work. Starting a family. The opposite of quitting.

Sure, I had my selfish motives for being here, but those were mixed with the good I saw by making changes to the past to help the future. And trying to help the Neanders, who'd been misrepresented since their fossil discovery in 1856.

The importance of this went far beyond me. I was actually changing the course of history in the world, as big-headed as that seemed.

Victoria, on the other hand, was in it only for herself. I knew her. Personal ambition at all costs. No concern about whatever unintended consequences would flow from her actions.

Victoria flapping her own butterfly wings would surely alter the future in unpredictable ways. And the longer she stayed the more uncertain that future would be.

But now she was here and there was nothing I could do about it. Or was there? Maybe I just needed to push her in the right direction.

I heard a shuffling and looked up to see Grandpa approaching us. He stepped into the log ring and took his time sitting down.

He was silent for a while, studying us and probably mulling over what he was going to say. Victoria had surreptitiously slipped the camera back into her pocket.

Finally, he raised a stumped finger, pointing up, and made a circle with it. Then he mumbled a few words, nodded at both of us, and stood back up to leave.

There would be a council meeting tomorrow. A meeting about us.

◆ ◆

Everyone was there, circling the fire. The entire band was either seated on the ground or on logs, or standing and leaning against the rock walls. They wanted to know what was going on. And so did I.

The cave smelled of smoke, cooked food, and human body odor. The usual. But there was an added scent. Maybe a feeling more than a smell. An edgy tension. Or maybe it was just me.

Grandpa stood next to the feather altar. It reached to his head and was made of branches bound with sinew. A ceremonial tower of sticks covered with Golden Eagle feathers. It was the symbol of power for this band, and Grandpa was its keeper.

Victoria and I sat on a log facing the altar. We were the subject of the meeting. We were the defendants.

"What's happening?" she asked, plainly nervous, her leg bouncing against mine.

"I think they're trying to decide what to do with us. This is pretty unprecedented, two white people from the future showing up."

"They know we're from the future?"

"Of course not. That would be impossible to explain. I'm just saying that they've never encountered something like this. I'm curious to see how they handle it."

Victoria was silent. I was sure she was plotting her next move. How she could exploit the situation.

I saw her put her hand in her pocket for the camera, but I nudged her and shook my head.

"Not now," I whispered. "Just pay attention."

Grandpa rapped a ceremonial staff on the ground three times. The meeting came to order.

"I'll try to translate as best I can," I said, "but you should be able to follow along by watching their body language. They're not subtle or ambiguous about it. It's all out in the open."

"Meaning not like us Sapiens?"

"Exactly."

I glanced at Victoria to see her nodding her head. She was taking it all in and committing it to memory. Most likely daydreaming about her upcoming lecture tour describing her trip to the Paleolithic past.

I reached under my covering and rubbed Carolyn's ring on its thong against my chest. I still called it her ring so I wouldn't forget her name.

Grandpa spoke for several minutes, frequently pointing to us. His tone was gentle and sounded sympathetic to my ear. He was probably suggesting that the band bring us into the fold somehow.

I had already proven myself, and Victoria represented multiple benefits, not the least of which was being a female of childbearing age, even if on the outside edge of that in their view. Grandpa was concerned about the future of the group, as he should have been.

When Grandpa finished, the Wrestler stood to speak. He was the one I had erroneously thought was fighting with Wren when I first arrived. The harder tone of his voice and his jabbing arm movements made a very different point. I caught the words *Minya* and *Nuh* several times. *Nuh* meant "bad" or "negative" or something similar.

He was speaking against us. He made several assertive hand gestures while looking directly at me. For whatever reason, he wanted us out.

Then Shorty stood and waited for the murmuring to stop. He said something to the Wrestler that made everyone laugh, then he pointed to Victoria. Even though I couldn't understand all his words, their meaning was hard to miss.

Shorty was Romeo giving his balcony scene speech to Juliet. He was wooing Victoria and making his case for having her become his third wife. It was a sophisticated performance from an archaic human, and I couldn't resist checking Victoria's reaction, which registered somewhere between astonishment and disgust.

Now it was our turn. Grandpa motioned to me, saying something I was sure was: "So make your case."

I was about to speak when a loud roar suddenly filled the cave, echoing off its hard walls.

The hair on my neck stood on end, and I spun around to see an enormous brown bear moving toward the narrowing point of the cave walls.

It was coming right at us.

26

The bear stopped just this side of the cave's pinch point near the feather piles, grunting and sniffing. It looked them over then turned back to us, rising up on its hind legs and letting out a fearsome roar that resulted in a chorus of high-pitched shrieks from everyone.

The bear must have been at least 1,000 pounds, and after shaking its huge body, it landed back on the cave floor, which quaked under its weight.

Before the bear could lift its head to roar again, I grabbed Victoria's arm and ran around the fire with the others. We were heading deeper into the cave and toward the sealed opening in the left wall that led to the burial chamber.

I had learned from Wren that this was the band's hard-to-reach safe room in case of extreme emergency.

And this was nothing if not an emergency.

While two men frantically pulled down the stones that obstructed the opening, I turned back to the bear. It had stopped near the fire to inspect the food and water left behind in the panic of fleeing.

I suddenly realized this was a cave bear, known to exist in Eurasia until around 24 kya when they went extinct. One of the most feared predators of the Pleistocene era, cave bears had no natural enemies except for the hungriest packs of wolves or hyenas. They were just too big and powerful.

But I never expected to see one this far south. I'd always associated them with the cold, northern latitudes. Yet, here was one in our cave!

I also remembered learning that cave bears got their name not from where they lived but from where they hibernated during the winter. And they didn't fully hibernate but, instead, went into a state called Torpor, where their heart rate dropped but they could still move around.

Which meant that this bear was not at its peak strength or power. It wanted nothing more than a cozy corner in a dark cave to lie down for a couple of months. But even in this weakened state, the bear would have no problem killing any bothersome humans—archaic or modern—that got in its way.

People were starting to cram into the narrow opening, but Victoria just stood there clicking away with her camera.

"It's a cave bear!" she said breathlessly.

"And this is no time for that," I shouted, grabbing her arm and pulling her toward the passageway.

She was resisting when Wren suddenly appeared and snatched the camera from Victoria's hand and threw it toward the fire.

"Go!" he said, pointing at the gap in the wall.

"Wait. My camera."

"Leave it!" I yelled, pushing her into the opening. "Do what I say. Now!"

I was about to enter the passageway when I took a quick look back and saw Grandpa. He had not fled with the rest of us. Instead, he stood his ground next to the fire and the feather altar.

He showed no fear as the bear moved slowly toward him, snuffling and grunting. He was distracting the animal to give everyone else time to escape. I was amazed by his courage.

Then I realized this was our chance.

I got the attention of both Wren and Shorty and motioned to them to join me. Soon, we were all crouched down and moving slowly against the back wall of the sleeping area on the far side of the fire. The bear would be least likely to see us here.

We had each picked up a thrusting spear and were now spread apart and stepping slowly toward the fire.

The bear had picked up the camera and was crunching it in its mouth when it must have sensed us because it suddenly roared and swiped Grandpa with a giant paw, sending him flying against the feather altar that crashed around him.

As though by some shared instinct, we three ran at the bear in the same moment without any signal between us. We just jumped the fire and attacked the giant animal while screaming our heads off.

Dodging its lethal front legs, we thrust our spears into the bear from every angle. As soon as it turned to face one attacker, another was on him from the other side. The bear spun around and around trying to fight us off with its long claws and large, curved teeth.

Blood from the bear—and us—was flowing freely now, and the fight devolved into a slow-motion battle with each side tiring and growing weaker by the minute.

When it seemed likely we would all perish, I caught movement in the corner of my eye.

Rabbit's hyena cub had broken loose and somehow managed to jump onto the bear's head, where it was frantically biting it with its tiny teeth and yipping and snarling at the same time.

This was too much for the bear. It shook off the cub and stood still on all fours.

It looked at us, let out a final roar, turned, and lumbered awkwardly toward the cave entrance. It had had enough.

I was betting we wouldn't see this bear again.

◆ ◆

"You bring," the Wrestler said, clearly angry and pointing at both me and Victoria. *"Nuh gook."* No good.

The whole group was back around the fire, cleaning up the mess and attending to the injured. Our wounds were not life-threatening but Grandpa was in bad shape, his chest ravaged by the bear.

The Wrestler was blaming us for the bear's appearance and rampage.

"Nuh gook," he kept repeating as two healing women cleaned our wounds and applied the poultices and wrappings we needed.

But Grandpa's injuries were the most serious and he soon had the healers tending exclusively to him. He had lost a lot of blood and I could see he was moving in and out of consciousness.

"What's that man saying?" Victoria asked, indicating the Wrestler. She was angry about the destroyed camera she held in her hand but equally distressed as she looked down at my bloodied left arm.

The bear had clawed it open and I could see bone in some places.

Thankfully, the effects of the pungent valerian root infusion I'd drunk were already taking effect. My anxiety was down and the pain wasn't so bad. But it certainly looked gruesome to see my arm mangled like this.

I said, "I think he's accusing us of bringing the bear through some sort of black magic that we possess. And maybe he's right."

Victoria gave me a fierce look. "Don't be absurd."

"Hey, wouldn't you question us if you were in their shoes?"

She pondered that while she looked around at the activity in the cave. The same cave she would be excavating 40,000 years later. I wondered what was going through her mind. And with no camera to record anything.

Everyone was busy either helping the injured or picking up or repairing the damages the bear had left in its wake. The feather altar would need major reconstruction.

"They do seem to have a cooperative spirit, don't they?" she finally said.

"That's one of my main conclusions from being here." I shifted my position so I could finish wrapping my arm in a soft fiber mesh that stank like rotten cheese. "They're a real community. They help each other out. They care."

"Oh, come on," she said, shaking her head. "Don't ascribe modern human attributes and qualities to these archaic humans. They are—don't forget—Neanderthals, after all. They're—"

"They're what? More primitive? Less evolved?"

She stared at me. "Well, technically, yes. They're not anatomically modern humans. We're the Sapiens here."

"And is that a good or bad thing?"

She studied me without speaking for a long moment. Then she stood, pocketing her smashed camera.

"Can I borrow your journal to make some notes?"

I chuckled. "Already working on your lecture?"

"*Our* lecture."

"Uh-huh."

I told her where I kept the journal and ink while I watched Brassy leave Grandpa's side and head in our direction.

Rabbit walked behind her pulling on the cub's leash. The growing hyena cub that had actually saved us.

Maybe there *was* a type of magic involved in all this. Me rescuing a hyena cub and the cub then returning the favor.

As Brassy approached us, I saw a look pass between her and Victoria. Curiosity? Disdain? Competitiveness? Jealousy?

Before I could decide, Victoria had walked off and Brassy sat next to me to examine my bandaged arm.

"Gook," she said simply. Good. It would heal.

And there was that smell again. Something Brassy applied to her skin as an insect repellent. With a distinctive minty scent that reminded me of citronella.

Which triggered a memory I'd almost forgotten. Of the beachside parties Carolyn and I used to have with our friends in L.A. Citronella candles placed around us in a circle to keep the mosquitoes away.

It was a good memory. But a sad one, too. Because I felt the image of Carolyn drifting away from me.

The cub bounced into my lap and started licking my face. Rabbit laughed and let go of the leash, putting his head against my good shoulder.

"Gook," he repeated in his small voice.

"You stay," Brassy said to me, pointing to Grandpa, who had his eyes open and was looking at us, smiling.

He had made his decision.

I wasn't going anywhere.

For now.

27

It was good to be out of the cave and doing something in the open air again.

Two weeks of cave-bound repairing and wound recovery had passed. My arm healed quickly with the poultice wraps, and I'd spent the time writing in my journal while Victoria continued to be astounded at being in the middle of the history she had spent her adult life studying.

She explored and inspected all the areas in the cave and also examined the neighboring caves. And she'd started communicating with any Neander who would sit with her. She was in anthropological heaven.

Since we had only one journal, I'd ripped out a few blank pages and presented them to her with a newly crafted, feather quill as a New Year's gift. She started writing notes immediately.

We were surely into January by now although the actual year was, naturally, in doubt. 40,001 BCE? 41,002 BCE? Trying to guess the year—or even the millennium—was a running joke between us.

But the discussion always turned serious whenever we brought up going back to our present. She was anxious to do it, but I was hesitant.

My initial thoughts had been to take what I could from 40 kya and turn my life around in 2019. But the more time I spent here, the more I questioned that idea. My hope for a family with Carolyn and our baby boy was shattered. It would never be. Which made the professional ambitions hollow. Empty.

What was I hurrying back for?

We'd started the expedition early. Shorty and Hand brought two of their wives to join me at the southern shoreline on a gathering mission. Victoria stayed behind in the cave to do more of her research.

We were there to collect limpets and mussels on the low tide. And anything else worth eating along the seashore.

It was a beautiful, brisk day—bright and clear—and we were well past the line of cairns on a narrow beach, with Africa was so close I could have swum to it.

When I suggested that in jest to the group, they all grew nervous and strongly shook their heads. As I'd already learned, they were honestly frightened by the idea of swimming.

Continuing with the joke, I took off my hide shoes and walked into the cold water up to my knees. I made swimming motions with my arms.

"Easy-peasy."

Shorty and Hand made it clear again. "No!" was the firm reply.

I had a sudden thought as I exited the water and watched a pair of dolphins arc their way past us just offshore. The sound of seagulls mixed with the breaking of small waves on the sand.

I pointed to the northern outline of Morocco and the Ceuta peninsula.

"Your people, they come from there?"

It took some time getting the idea across, even drawing a map in the sand at our feet, but they finally understood my question.

"No," Shorty said. "Come there." He pointed north.

This lined up with the latest theories of how Neanderthals had evolved in central and western Eurasia, then expanded into southwest Europe and ultimately ended up in their last refuges in southern Iberia.

I'd always wondered why archaic humans hadn't simply crossed the Strait of Gibraltar from Africa and short-circuited tens of thousands of years of history to arrive in Europe. Looking into Wren and Brassy's terrified faces offered the simplest answer: they were petrified by large bodies of water.

The sun was behind us as we worked our way east

along the curving shoreline. Gulls dive-bombed for small fish offshore while we gradually filled our woven pouches with all manner of gastropods: snails, slugs, mussels, and cone-shaped limpets.

The growing smell of the dying creatures was overpowering, but that was a small price to pay for the food value we were collecting.

The wind had come up after we turned back toward the Rock, and as we trudged our way through hissing sand dunes and in and out of small stands of stone pine and olive trees, we stopped talking and simply put our heads down and focused on our feet.

We were passing a small lake when I had another idea.

I removed my shoes and stepped into the water. It wasn't that cold. The lake was shallow enough that the day's sun had warmed it up to a tolerable temperature. I had swum in water much colder than this and thought I would try to approach their fear of water with one last attempt.

It was time for a swim lesson.

The men refused outright but the women were curious and interested. I soon had a volunteer.

She was Hand's wife, who was short and a little plump. If any Neander could float, it would be her. I nicknamed her Chubby.

When I pointed to her thick tunic, subtly suggesting that she would be walking home wet and shivering, she didn't hesitate. Chubby took off the covering, threw it at Hand, and waded into the water stark naked.

Carefully watching where I put my hands, I went through a condensed version of the basic swim lesson steps: blowing bubbles, rotating the head to breathe, kicking, and practice sinking under.

The goal was to get her comfortable in the water. To not be afraid of it. To feel safe.

I knew it would take more than a 30-minute lesson, but at the end, Chubby was smiling broadly and splashing water at me. She was enjoying herself, and that's what counted.

If I could teach her, I could teach others. And they, others. And someday in the future, these Neanders could have another option for fleeing, fighting, or migrating.

We were gathering our things and preparing to leave the lake when I heard a sound. It was a whistle coming from somewhere above us. And echoed by another at a different spot.

The lake was in a shallow depression of coarse sand and reeds. Sand dunes ringed the lake, and I suddenly saw the shape of a man rising over a dune. Spinning around I saw more.

We were surrounded by a group of six men.

The first man started walking down the dune toward us. I recognized him instantly. He was the dark Sapien leader from Malaga. And he was hitting his club against his other hand in a clear sign.

He was ready to fight.

The Malaga leader stopped at the bottom of the dune and yelled out something.

Immediately, spears stuck in the sand all around our group, only missing us because of the quick reflexes of Hand and Shorty, who pushed me and others out of the line of fire at the last moment. Nothing struck us but the message was clear: we were not having a discussion or a meeting. This was an attack.

We had brought only one long spear, blades, and my atlatl and quiver of short spears for defense. We were anticipating a threat from animals, not from people. And we were three men and two women to their six men. We were in trouble.

Quickly looking around, I noticed that the Malaga Neanders were also advancing down the dunes toward us, but they were farther behind the two dark Sapiens who were approaching from opposite sides. The Neanders were either showing their subordination to the Sapiens, or they wanted to see what their leaders would do first.

Either way, these Malaga Neanders were followers, not leaders, and maybe—just maybe—they didn't see this as a necessary fight. And I wondered how loyal they were.

A thought flashed.

"Come!" I shouted to the others in my group as I stepped back into the lake's waters. "Follow me."

Shorty and Hand were perplexed and refused to move, but the two women seemed to understand what I was doing and pushed the two men into the water with them.

Soon, we all stood in waist-deep water watching the attackers converge at the lake's western shore. I motioned for everyone to stand apart so we wouldn't bunch up and present a single mass target.

The sun was low to our left and the wind was dying down. The only sounds were the far-off calls of gulls and the increased murmuring of the Malaga Neanders who looked more confused by the minute.

We were now two distinct groups facing off against each other. One in the water, one on dry land.

The Sapien leader called out what sounded like an order to rush at us, but that only increased the nervousness of the Neanders. As I'd guessed, they were afraid of the water, too.

The leader, his anger raging across his face, began to beat nearby Neanders with his club, ordering them to move into the water and attack us. The other Sapien moved to the back of their group and started pushing everyone forward.

But the Neanders pushed back and resisted, some falling down rather than entering the lake.

Finally, the Sapien leader had had enough. After signaling to his partner, he splashed into the shallow water and headed straight for us. The other was right behind him. Both men were cursing and had their clubs raised and ready for battle.

I gripped one of my short spears and moved to the front of our group.

Instead of panicking at the sight of the approaching danger—or slipping into one of my old OCD patterns of tapping or pressing—I brought up a deeply buried part of my childhood.

As a frequent victim of violence in my early life, I had developed two types of responses to threats. One, I withdrew into myself and my passive coping mechanisms—my OCD behaviors. Two, I went in the opposite direction. I'd turn the tables on victimhood and become the aggressor. I was willing—eager, even—to fight back.

Watching the Sapien leader approach, alternative two clicked in. My body automatically slowed down and I retreated into a state of quiet readiness. Like a crouching panther poised to strike.

As soon as he was close enough for me to see his flaring nose and hear his throaty breath, the man swung his club, but I stepped to the side to avoid it and struck him hard between the eyes with my fist.

He stumbled back, shocked, holding his head. He'd probably never been counterattacked. Which gave me my opening.

I lunged at the man and drove my spear deep into his neck.

His eyes widened as he teetered backward, clutching for the spear I held firmly in place.

He slowly sank down in the water to his knees, blood fanning out in all directions. The water was over his shoulders and he sputtered unintelligible words while his glazed eyes never left mine.

Then he let out a final gasp and slipped under.

I turned to watch Hand and Shorty chase the other Sapien away and then return. I nodded to them and looked to the shoreline where the Malaga Neanders stood in rigid silence staring at me.

Their leader's body suddenly popped to the surface and rolled onto its back. The man's face was contorted with an open-mouthed grimace and with eyes fixed on the sky.

The adrenaline from fighting was ebbing as I looked up at my group and saw the startled reaction on their faces.

I was no longer just the strange man who wrote notes in his journal and taught them funny words.

I was a warrior. I was *their* warrior.

28

Like chickens shadowing each other, the four Malaga Neanders followed us back to the cave. Their Sapien leaders were gone, and they seemed more than happy to be with others like themselves.

The isolation of the Neanderthal bands was evident as the two groups laughed together in their attempts to communicate.

And we did our best to welcome the newcomers, offering them food and water, and finding them places to sleep.

Once everyone was settled in for the night, Victoria pulled me aside and we walked to the cave entrance to talk. Sitting next to a deep vertical crack in the rock just inside the cave's opening with a bright moon and a million stars lighting up the ground, I could see that she was nervous.

Victoria asked, "What happened out there?"

"We ran into that other Neanderthal group and, well, things got tense."

"How tense?"

I looked into her alarmed eyes that gleamed with moonlight.

"I killed their Sapien leader. And they drove another one away."

Her mouth opened and hung there before she spoke.

"You what? You killed someone? You, who warned me about the consequences of changing the past?"

"I had no choice. It was him or me."

She shook her head. "And what about your *discrepancies*? How this will change things back in our time?"

"Honestly, I'm not sure. But I see a way to help these people. And maybe help the future."

"What are you talking about? We know exactly what happens to the Neanderthals. They go extinct. We're just not sure why. And there's nothing you or I can do about it."

She put her hand on my arm. "But we can go back and tell a fuller story of what it was really like. *That's* what we can do to help them. That's what I plan to do. And soon."

I let that sink in as I stared out into the night. I had gotten used to not seeing any lights shining on the African shore, and the thought of not rushing back was now establishing itself.

"What if I don't go back right away? What if you do but I stay a little longer?"

"A little longer? For how long? And why?"

The plan was still jumbled in my mind, but I knew that I could have a direct impact here. I could prepare this group for what was coming: another onslaught of men from the north. The Malaga Sapien leader had already hinted at it.

I could improve the chances of these Neanders surviving. And that could possibly help the future of my world in 2019. A key change here or there could ripple forward to our own time.

Genetic research had recently discovered that some Neanderthal genes had a direct impact on modern peoples' LDL cholesterol levels, body fat accumulation, how badly we sunburn, and even sleep time preference, or whether someone is a morning person or a night owl.

Those effects were already known and proven by modern science in 2018. What about other changes that hadn't yet happened in the future?

"Maybe I can bring the two Neander groups together somehow to help them," I said. "Teach them more things. Improve their skills."

Victoria sighed. "Look, I can't make you do anything, but you're dreaming. You know you can't change the future."

"Oh, yes I can. I already have."

"That's what you say. But realistically—"

"That's what I know. You haven't experienced it yet, but you will."

She gave me an unconvinced look, but before either of us could speak the hyena cub suddenly bounded between us and started licking my face.

I pushed the cub away, laughing, and Rabbit was quickly there to control it. The cub had outgrown the leash.

"Gud kauta," he said proudly. His hyena.

"Yes, it is," I said, glancing at Victoria. "The first domesticated hyena in the world, I'm guessing. Who knows what could happen now."

Victoria just stared at me. I knew she didn't believe me about changing the future, but I was becoming committed to it.

"And Carolyn?" she asked, glancing around. "A lot of explosion specialists and crime scene investigators here?"

That hurt. I had tried to push Carolyn's certain death out of my mind.

"No. But I *am* planning to go back. Just not now."

I saw her look up, so I turned. It was Brassy. Her hair was less tangled than I remembered, and her eyes flitted between me and Victoria.

"You gook?" she asked me.

Victoria sniggered. "Ah, now I see." She lifted an eyebrow at me.

"You gook?" Brassy repeated, narrowing her eyes at Victoria.

"I gook," I said, with the biggest smile I could manage.

• ◆

We spent the next week preparing the cave for the Malaga Neanders. More space was made in the sleeping chamber, more skins allocated. The two bands would be merging with the Malagas coming to Meredith's Cave.

The leadership council had voted, and I was the deciding vote. Wren voted yes, Brassy no, and Grandpa was too sick to make up his mind. He was still gravely injured and hallucinating.

I had argued that joining forces—and increasing numbers, from 11 to 24—was the right move. There was strength in numbers, and I used the recent fight at the lake as my evidence that the group needed to prepare for more violent encounters.

I also knew that one potential factor in the downfall of Neanderthals as a species could have been their inability to form large social groups. Larger groups allow more opportunities for innovation and for more social connections that can provide help in times of need. Merging the two bands would aid that.

Two of the Malagas stayed while the other two went back to fetch the rest of their group. And I learned more about why they had so readily agreed to this change.

The two Sapiens had come from the north and had, over time, wrestled the band's leadership away and become tyrannical despots. The Neanders had become the slaves of the Sapiens, who were vicious in maintaining their control.

There had been an attempted uprising early on, but the Sapiens had crushed it with treachery, corruption, and violent force. From then on, any dissent was immediately punished, usually by death.

Near the end of the eighth day the rest of the Malaga Neanders arrived, and the cave buzzed with greetings and commotion. I had suggested that one of our group pair up with one of theirs and become their guide and companion. After some initial hesitation, the Meredith cavers took on the task with enthusiasm.

Groups of two moved around the cave eating and drinking and talking. I was proud of my Neanderthals.

Beyond their initial—and expected—apprehension and disorientation, this new group seemed little different from ours. They looked and acted the same. Their speech had that sing-song quality, and the language was similarly simplistic with lots of expressive signing involved. I would have new recruits for my language classes.

As the first night ended, everyone retired to the sleeping chamber. My spot was now near and equidistant from Brassy and Victoria. There had been some not-so-subtle wrangling between the two women over this positioning.

I could understand Victoria's wanting to be close to someone she knew, but Brassy's boldness and obvious interest made me a little uncomfortable. My lying between them seemed like the best compromise.

After all the murmuring and movements ended, the night's communal singing started. From my vantage point, I could see the newcomers hesitate at first but then gradually join in with their own voices. The ritual was not unfamiliar to them.

Victoria had marveled over this discovery of nocturnal chanting, and I now caught her looking directly at me from under her animal skin. She held out a hand to display something to me. It was the pierced shell she'd used to make the time transition.

She jiggled her hand to make sure I was watching. Then she mouthed the word *tomorrow* and pointed a finger at me.

She was going back.

◆ ◆

Dense fog covered the plain down to the cairns and the lake. A shrouded sun, barely visible as a bright blotch in the fog, chilled the wet air while we hiked at a fast pace trying to generate body heat.

The lake water would be cold, so the warmer we were when we reached it, the better.

"I'm glad to be out of that smoky, sweaty cave," Victoria said, walking next to me. "I don't know how you can stand it."

"You get used to it."

Our breathing was synchronized as we negotiated the dunes, brush thickets, and pine stands.

"Explain to me again why you're not going back with me."

I let the reasons tumble in my head.

"It's too soon. I want to finish up some things first."

"Like what?"

"I want to make sure the other Neander band is fully integrated."

She stopped me. "But why? You're not going to change anything. You do understand that trying to alter the outcome for the Neanderthals is a lost cause, right?"

"I'm not so sure about that. I think I can help these Neanders. And our world, too. I know it sounds a little off—"

"*Off* is the milder form of the description I was thinking of." But she grinned and the tension lifted.

"Look," she said. "You have your agenda and I have mine. If you want to stay a little longer, that's up to you. But I need to get back. You understand, right?"

I studied her for a moment, then nodded. "I do."

We reached the lake at midday. The fog had mostly burned off, leaving only wisps of white mist dancing in the sunlight.

Victoria stepped into the lake and shrieked, *"It's freezing!"*

I chuckled as I took her hide tunic. "Don't worry, you won't be in long. And you'll have a hot shower waiting for you at the hotel."

She wore the same clothes she'd arrived in: blue-jean shorts under a man's white button-down shirt, now dirty and frayed.

She had added a small oiled bag of anthropological evidence tied around her waist, like a fanny pack. Inside were a handaxe, another shell necklace, and pigment blocks and tips of drawing sticks from the art gallery, which had made her gasp when she first saw it. And her busted camera.

She had also folded up several pages of her journal notes in the bag.

"Do you have the totem?" I asked her.

She patted the breast pocket of her shirt.

I had cut off a piece of the rawhide shoelace—her link to the other life—and she had strung it through the shell and tied it off in a knot.

"You're absolutely sure you don't want to come back with me?" she asked. She was shivering.

"I'm sure. Not now. And you better get going before you turn to ice."

I pointed. "Swim to the center of the lake. Touch the totem then dive down with a clear mind. No thoughts. No worries."

"No thoughts. No worries," she repeated with a slight nod of her head.

After a moment's pause, she gripped my forearm and gave me a final look that combined sadness and anticipation. Then she turned and shuffled out to where the water was up to her waist.

She hesitated, then plunged in and started swimming away. Once she reached the center of the lake, she stopped, looked up, and waved to me.

I waved back and saw her take a couple of deep breaths before she dropped her head and started her dive. I watched until her feet disappeared under the water.

Victoria was gone. Hopefully, back to our 2019.

PART FOUR

Are You Gook?

29

There was no sign of Tom after two weeks, and Victoria wasn't waiting.

She had been careful to send the artifacts she'd brought back to a different lab for testing. Not the regular one used for the dig. And she was purposefully vague in the documentation that went with the items. No details on where they'd been found, or even by whom. She said it was for a colleague who wished to maintain his privacy.

And her few pages of notes from Tom's journal were deliberately hidden away. She wasn't ready to reveal them yet.

But she couldn't stop the leaks and rumors about her finding the Neanderthal hand and ring from spreading. She'd been fielding so many calls from scientists and publications that she stopped answering her phone. Or even looking at her emails. That editor from Science Alive *had been especially bothersome by constantly asking where Tom was.*

However, one thing she'd done was to check if he was right about things changing because of their actions in the past. And sure enough, they had.

The museum director was a different person. A woman. Even the name of the restaurant where they ate had changed. And the street it was on.

There were other changes as well, but she didn't have the time to fully investigate them. What she had to do was find more proof of the travel through time. Something that tied her or Tom directly to 40 kya. That was the knock-out news. That's what would make her a shooting star.

The mangled camera was useless, and the handwritten notes weren't enough. The chain of custody could not be proven or linked to a contemporary archeological excavation, which was the key.

She needed more. Something definitive.

Skeptics online were already claiming that the skeletal remains and the ring in the cave were somehow faked. That maybe she was a fake. And with her academic future on the line, that kind of talk had to be stopped.

She stood at the cave entrance and looked out at the Mediterranean. A heavy mist clung to the coast of Africa, but above that, she could see the first stars of twilight appearing. The moon was full and bright, and her mind went back to the night when the two of them sat nearby and talked about traveling forward to the present. He was already hedging about it then. What was that man thinking?

Carolyn's body had finally been found, washed up on a shore to the north of the Rock. But Tom didn't know that. Or did he? Of course, he would have guessed. Known in his heart. And maybe that was one of the reasons he wasn't back yet.

She focused on the journal. It would have what she needed. Tom had been diligent about recording everything. Full descriptions in words that were complemented by his sketches and drawings.

It would all be there. And with ink and other stratigraphic deposits surrounding the journal that would be datable to the period. But it had to be discovered as part of an official dig.

She thought harder. If something had happened to Tom, he would have been careful to make sure the journal would eventually be found and excavated. Hidden someplace where he would know she'd look in connection with the current dig. But where?

30

As I walked back to the cave from seeing off Victoria, my feelings of isolation and loneliness collided with their opposites: companionship and belonging.

Here I was, an imperfect modern man with plenty of problems and hang-ups going back to my Neanderthal society. Where I was not only a member but a leader.

Could this situation be any more extraordinary?

Yes, it could. I could turn around, leave 40 kya behind, and follow Victoria back to 2019. If it even was 2019. Or the same 2019.

Maybe Victoria and I had already changed that version of the timestream. Maybe there was less global violence. Or maybe World War III was about to erupt.

I knew one thing. Carolyn was most likely dead.

Along with our baby, Devin. That wasn't changing no matter what I did.

So maybe I could follow a different path. I could re-enter my new community at the cave and focus on helping them. For a little while.

Stop thinking about me and my troubles and start being more generous. I had a lot to offer. I had expertise. I had knowledge that skirted the edge of magic from their point of view.

I could give my Neanders a leg up. I could improve their chances of survival. And that could flow down through the millennia.

Maybe.

I'd already told Victoria that what I was doing was temporary. A pause before I followed her back. I let that thought hover over my mind like an eagle hanging in the wind looking down for rabbits as I walked up the last patch of loose scree to the cave entrance.

Wren was waiting for me at the opening with a look of relief on his face.

"You come," he said matter-of-factly before he turned to enter the cave.

I followed him back to the sleeping chamber where Grandpa was lying.

At least a half dozen Neanders were circled around him, and most were crying. Including Brassy, who gave me a look that appeared to mix happiness with anguish.

Grandpa saw me, looked up, and motioned with his hand for me to approach. As I did, I could see that his chest was enlarged. And in between the different wrappings I saw puffy skin. He was badly infected. Probably sepsis.

I kneeled at his side and noticed that his breathing was rapid and shallow. His skin had a ghostly pale tinge, and he was shivering uncontrollably.

"Tum Kuk," he whispered, beckoning me with his fingers.

I leaned in closer and could smell fecal odor on his breath.

"You . . ." He touched a bony finger on my forearm. "You gook."

I smiled, conscious that everyone around us was silent, listening intently.

"You *gook per mooka.*"

I blinked and stared at him. He was saying that I was good for the Neanders. He was giving me his blessing. His approval.

He grabbed my skin covering and pulled me closer. His breath was hot, and each puff came out with a deep wheezing sound.

"You stay per mooka?" he asked.

I looked up into a circle of Neanderthal faces staring down at me. They were motionless, waiting for my response.

I looked into the old man's rheumy eyes and stroked his hand. "I stay per mooka."

He smiled and closed his eyes. I was telling a dying old man what he wanted to hear.

◆ ◆

Grandpa died in the night and we spent the next day carefully following the rituals. His body was placed in the most prominent niche in the burial chamber. Multiple chants were started, each more soaring and beautiful than the one before. I found myself wiping away tears throughout the day.

Grandpa had been the symbolic and spiritual leader of the group for as long as anyone could remember, and his departure left a yawning vacuum. Who could take his place?

It was decided that the rest of the leadership council—Wren, Brassy, and me—would take over Grandpa's role as a team. At least for a while.

During the day I'd paid attention to the Malaga Neanders, who were careful to stand back and out of the way while still participating in the funeral ceremony.

One of the men seemed more moved by the day's events than the others, and I noticed several Malagas deferring to him. He was a leader of some kind who had gone back to fetch the others and bring them to the cave. So I pulled him aside after the evening meal of roasted rabbit and roots boiled with hot rocks in a turtle shell. I wanted some information.

Holding gourds of pine needle tea, we walked to a shallow alcove in the cave past the narrowing point. We sat facing each other as several small birds flew in and out of the cave, twittering in the falling light.

The man was about the same age as Wren—early 30s?—although not as tall. He had a full head of long, black hair and a dense beard. Similar to Wren, he had slightly darker skin but his eyes were brown, not blue. And he was well-muscled. Thickly built. A typical Neanderthal.

He was already participating in my language classes so I hoped our communication would get results.

To start things off, I held out my gourd cup to touch his as a form of toast. He didn't understand my intention and kept the gourd close to his chest. Then I tried again, extending my gourd to his at the same time I said the word *toast*, smiling and nodding.

He finally let his gourd touch mine and I broke into a broad grin showing my appreciation. He responded by touching gourds again and beaming.

"Tust," he said tentatively.

I doubted the subtle symbology of beverage toasting that unites individuals and forms a bond of good wishes was fully understood by him, but he seemed to follow what I was doing.

We got comfortable exchanging words and ideas on an elementary basis before I moved the conversation in the direction I wanted. I needed to confirm my suspicions.

"The Minya from the north," I started, pointing up to the ceiling. "They come? They *puk*?"

He tilted his head and scrunched up his large eyebrows. He was unsure.

I extended both arms straight out and wiggled my fingers up and down, gradually pulling the hands closer to me. I was trying to signal a large group coming to us.

"Many Minya. Coming here? From the north?"

I repeated the motion and the man started to nod. He was about to say something when Wren and Brassy suddenly appeared and joined us on the dirt floor with their own gourds of tea. Everyone exchanged smiles and head nods.

I motioned for the man to say what he was going to say.

He looked at each of us in turn then started extending his arms in my direction, wiggling his fingers as I had done.

"Minya puk nik," he said as best I could make out. *"Minya puk nik,"*

"Minya come from north," Wren and Brassy both said almost simultaneously.

So it was true.

The Sapiens were coming for us.

31

I had no idea how much time we had, but I wasn't taking anything for granted. We needed to get serious about the approaching threat.

The next week was devoted to organization and preparation. But this was not a spontaneous conclusion reached by people with limited practice in forward planning. Instead, I had to take control and focus everyone's attention on the threat and the discrete steps needed to address it.

The first order of business was to add someone from the other group to the leadership council. The one I had sat with—I nicknamed him Malaga—was the obvious choice. No one disagreed, and he was pleased although unsure of what he was supposed to do.

For me—and I was no military strategist but had

seen dozens of war movies—the next step was to inventory and increase our vital supplies and resources. That meant food and water and weapons. So I did what any military commander would do: I delegated.

Brassy would organize the food and water, and she went at it with enthusiasm, directing the cooking of food and the collecting of water. In fact, and as her nickname implied, she went over the top.

She immediately began bossing the other women around—especially the new Malaga women—giving loud orders and verbally scolding any woman who moved too slowly.

There were so many complaints about Brassy's behavior that I had to take her aside for a chat.

We sat just outside the cave entrance under a shallow ledge that kept off a light rain. At first, she looked confused about why I had pulled her away. Then I saw a change in her expression.

A suggestive smile spread across her face while she moved closer to me on the hard sand. She leaned in and put a hand on my knee.

It took me only a moment to realize she was coming onto me. And I wasn't sure what to do. I'd been the recipient of approaches and flirtations from women over the years, but never like this. I was being hit on by a Neanderthal!

I reacted instinctively by moving her hand off my knee and scooching myself away a few inches.

I shook my head. "No, I want to talk to you about

something. Something else."

I must have blushed because she cocked her head and drew up the corners of her mouth into a smug smile. But she also understood the message and nodded.

"You talk," she said, leaning back and emphasizing her ample breasts with undeniable intention.

And when she did this, I was embarrassed to feel the tightness of my shorts over my crotch. And her quick eyes saw it too, before raising to meet my embarrassment.

"Enough," I said before I jumped to my feet and started pacing back and forth. "You need to be nicer to the others. Don't be so hard."

Feeling stupid, I sat back down.

"Be soft with others. They help you."

"Suft," she said, quieting her voice.

I nodded. "Yes, quiet and soft. You get more that way."

It seemed I was getting through as I watched her eyes move down from mine to my chest.

She reached her hand out to touch the ring that bulged under my skin covering.

"Ring," she said with confidence.

The ring that had started all this.

◆ ◆

Weapons were next. What could we use to defend ourselves from a Sapien attack? And where would we do this defending?

Wren and I started with an inventory of our weapons. Using my journal, I made a list of every blade, spear, and club our group possessed. I added my atlatl and clutch of short spears.

Malaga immediately caught on to this and added what his group had to the inventory. But then he surprised me.

"*Shat,*" he said as he held out a bent wooden stick for my inspection with one hand and flashed five fingers twice with the other. Ten in total.

So these were the legendary "throwing sticks" I had read about in my research of archaic human weaponry. They apparently dated back a couple of million years to *Homo erectus* and were used as a high-speed throwing tool in a hunt. And, I presumed, in a battle.

I gripped the shat and studied it. It was carved flat from a bent branch and reminded me of an elongated boomerang with a sharp edge. The longer side was probably two feet, and the shorter one was less than a foot in length. It weighed about a pound.

My Neanders didn't use these for some reason, but I was determined to find out what we could do with this new—to us—weapon.

"Let's test it," I said to both men with no response.

"Test," I repeated while I held up the stick and made a mock throwing motion with it, then pointed to the cave entrance.

Wren and Malaga both looked at each other and

smiled, nodding.

"Test," Wren said as he and Malaga started walking.

We found a suitable spot about 15 yards downhill from the cave opening. The ground was a mix of loose scree and hardened sand, and it was relatively flat.

I stacked up a pile of empty water gourds to the side of the cave opening and explained that we would try to hit the gourds with the shat. First one to make a successful strike would be rewarded with a full gourd of alcoholic neek.

That brought a smile to both men. Now they were motivated.

Wren went first. He was accurate with long spears, but by the way he was handling the shat, this would be different.

He drew the stick back and awkwardly hurled it at the gourds. It fell short and off to the side. He had missed by a mile, and his embarrassed face showed it.

I was up next. I felt the weight of the throwing stick in my hand then lifted it behind my head and threw it with my best baseball arm.

The shat made a whirring sound as it flew before it struck the cliff wall near the cave, but still wide of the target. My throw was better than Wren's but not by much.

Malaga was barely keeping in his laughter, and now it was his turn.

He wasted no time after he got the shat back.

Holding the stick in his right hand, he turned his

body at an angle to the target, left foot forward. Then in one smooth movement, he leaned his body backward, lifted up his throwing arm even with his head, and launched the weapon with a practiced power.

The shat struck the gourd pile dead center with a loud crash and sent the broken pieces flying every which way.

Both Wren and I were awestruck, but Malaga just grinned back at us.

"Test gook," he said simply as he trotted off to retrieve the new weapon.

We would start training with the shat.

◆ ◆

The next day was for reconnoitering our position and our defenses.

Geographically, the Gibraltar cave complex and the entire peninsula were very different 40,000 years ago from what the maps of 2019 showed. The Rock—a peaking north-to-south ridge of Jurassic limestone—was still the dominating element, but the peninsula itself was much wider. A sloping plain extended several kilometers in all directions, especially to the east.

A wider peninsula was harder to defend so I decided that the best option was to set up an early warning system. If we could spot the invaders in advance, we would have an advantage in fleeing or defending. At least that was my theory, and everyone was now looking to me as the master strategist.

I established two observation outposts on the extreme north and south peaks. These would be manned 24/7 with rotating observers pulling roughly six-hour shifts. And they wouldn't be just men. In fact, the Neander women seemed more adept at noticing subtle changes in the environment. They were the first to see prey moving through the bush during hunts.

And I was also counting on a key difference between Neanderthals and Sapiens for our benefit: Neanders had bigger eyes and better vision at night.

While Neanderthal brains were similar in size to those of modern humans, the fossil evidence indicated that more of their brain was dedicated to vision and body control, leaving less room for other things, like higher-level thinking.

Most paleoanthropologists treated this idea of enhanced night vision as an unverified theory, but I had witnessed it first-hand.

I was continually surprised when something—or someone—was pointed out to me at night that I couldn't see. I had learned to simply wait when I was told "here he comes," and soon, there he'd be. It was a little unnerving at first, but I got used to it, and now I was going to exploit this difference if I got the chance.

So there was no need for me to take a turn as a nighttime lookout. I would be hopeless compared to any half-asleep Neander.

It made the most sense for me to stay at the main

base of operations: the cave. I was now a general calling the shots for my troop of Neanderthal soldiers.

And while we had different escape routes for fleeing, the cave would be our final fortress, if need be. We knew all the passageways, tunnels, and chambers. We could defend one after another, taking appropriate countermeasures where we could.

And we would set traps. I had already outlined three types in my journal, and I assigned different groups to the tasks of creating them.

Having considered the strengths of the Neanders compared to the Sapiens—more muscular power, better night vision, an innate emotional bond—I felt that we could hold our own in a battle for our lives. Ready to engage or retreat, to hide or escape, to attack or fall back.

If it came down to it, the cave would be our Alamo, and we would fight to the bitter end.

32

More than a week of being in charge of strategy and preparations had taken a toll on me. I was tired.

I also led the daily training sessions where we practiced how to take our defensive positions when the alarm was sounded that the Sapiens were coming, or worse, had arrived.

I needed a break.

I climbed up on the Rock to a small pinnacle above the cave with a flat spot that looked eastward. I wanted to quiet my chaotic mind and be alone for a while.

I found a log and sat on it with my face turned to the rising sun. The only sound was the wind rustling through the scrub bushes around me.

With my eyes closed and feeling the warmth of the late-January sun spreading over my face, I started my finger-pressing routine. It seemed that my OCD behaviors decreased with each day I spent in 40 kya, and I needed my calming routines less and less. So this was more like a form of meditation for me.

But now, sitting here without the distractions and busyness of the cave, all my doubts, fears, and feelings of bitterness about Carolyn came washing over me. Did I really think I could change things in this world—or in the future—for the better? Was I deluding myself?

I heard movement behind me and opened my eyes, shading them with my hand. Before I could turn, I heard the yips and yelps of the hyena cub that was suddenly in my lap, licking my face.

I laughed and started pushing the hyena away. My doubts were evaporating with each squirm and twitch of the cub.

Rabbit then appeared and started yelling at the cub, futilely trying to control it.

"Come sit with me," I said to Rabbit, patting the log.

Rabbit sat and grabbed the cub's neck, pulling the growing animal down to the ground.

The hyena, cackling from its open mouth, was enjoying the attention and soon lulled itself to lie quietly at our feet.

It would have made a nice painting or photograph from the rear. A man from the future sitting on a log with a Neanderthal boy and his pet hyena, staring at a Pleistocene landscape full of wonders and surprises.

I rubbed Rabbit's head and looked out to Africa

and the distant sea that would one day be called the Mediterranean.

Maybe things weren't so bad after all. Maybe I was doing something to help a Neanderthal boy and his pet and his people.

Maybe there was a better future ahead for them. And for me.

◆ ◆

The optimism I'd experienced two days earlier abruptly ended with the arrival of an outpost runner. The Sapiens were here! They were spotted just before sunrise marching south on the plain below the northern edge of the Rock.

I shouted to Wren and Malaga and sprinted out of the cave with them. We were heading for the same pinnacle that overlooked the plain. I wanted to see this with my own eyes.

The sun was a full hand above the horizon by the time we reached the peak. We all hid behind a barrier of thorn bushes and watched as the slow-moving group came into view from our left.

By their long-limbed movements, I spotted 10 of the Sapiens, but there was also a small group of shorter, stockier Neanderthals in front of them.

I heard Malaga gasp. "Mooka!" he shrieked.

Based on my best interpretation of the words that flowed from his mouth, this was a left-over group of his people from the Malaga community. They could have been away on a hunting trip, or he had missed them when he traveled back to bring everyone down to join us in the cave. And the Sapiens had evidently traveled south by way of Malaga to round up these people.

But what concerned me most was the way this Neanderthal group was being treated. Not only did they appear to have ropes around their necks, stringing them all together, but the Sapiens were continually beating them with clubs and using what looked like whips on them to keep them moving.

Malaga was beside himself with rage at seeing this, and I had to hold him back from rushing forward and revealing our hiding spot. Wren was also upset by this overt display of brutal authority and domination.

We all knew the Malagas had been slaves of the two Sapiens, but these new Sapiens seemed to be bringing pointed attention to this fact. It almost felt like a ransom ploy. *We'll release our hostages if you show yourselves.*

The intruders and their captives finally stopped at a point in line with our perch and the cave mouth. They were far below us, but we could clearly see their movements in the mid-morning sunlight.

All of a sudden, the Sapiens began shouting and the Neanders started running away as a group, still tied together by ropes.

I watched as the Sapiens took their time fitting darts to their spear throwers and running after the Neanders, laughing and shouting. They were hunting them down like animals.

Once they were in range, the Sapiens launched their spears into the backs and legs of the tiring Neanders.

One by one they fell, dead or injured. And because they were still tied together, each victim took down at least two more with him.

Soon, the Sapiens were on top of the Neanders, either clubbing them to death or slitting their throats.

When they were finished and all the Neanders lay still on the blood-covered plain, the Sapiens as a group turned and looked up at the Rock.

What we on our perch—and anyone watching from the cave entrance below—had just witnessed was a show. A show for us. A show of strength. A show of *Homo sapiens* evil.

◆ ◆

We took a back route down the Rock and entered a rear opening to the cave system. There were two escape routes from Meredith's Cave like this, and both now had permanent guards watching them.

The three of us ran at full speed through the labyrinth of passageways, corridors, and rooms until we emerged in the cave's main chamber.

I could instantly see that everyone was scared. Some huddled together in small groups around the fire while several of the stronger men—including Shorty, Hand, and the Wrestler—were already at work finishing the barrier wall at the cave entrance.

Earlier, I'd imagined a sort of rock dam that could block the cave opening in case of extreme emergency. And I started a work project to create it. Big stones, including some manageable boulders, had been brought from the outside to build up a pyramidal blockade of the cave's mouth.

Over days of constant work, the barrier had grown higher and higher. To the point where it was now impossible to leave or enter the cave without climbing over the large rock mound.

The edges of the barrier reached the top of the cave opening, but a small dip remained in the center to allow some access and for viewing. When this last piece was closed, we would be sealed in the cave.

I carefully worked my way up the sloped side of the mound. A slip or a fall here could easily result in a twisted ankle or a broken leg, so I took my time.

When I reached the top, I pulled over one of the thick reed mats that were there to cushion against the sharp rocks.

This would be the main lookout position from inside the cave. There were still several scouts scattered outside in well-hidden locations, but this would be where the top general—me—would be making his important decisions.

And I felt the full weight of the responsibility on my shoulders. This combined group of two-dozen Neanders—including children—was looking to me to come to the right conclusions. Me. A fairly screwed-up science reporter turned time traveler.

I seriously wondered if I was up to the task.

I instinctively reached to my main comfort item: Carolyn's ring.

The ring—still dangling from its thong under my mantle—equally grounded me to this place and reminded me that I had another life in the future. But it was the *now* that fully occupied my thoughts.

I looked out from the elevated roost to survey the scene. And what I saw was not what I was expecting.

The sun was up as high as it would get today, arcing across a cobalt blue sky with no clouds in sight. But what separated the sky into two parts was a thin column of black smoke lifting straight up from the plain. I followed the smoke down to its point of origin and smelled something familiar.

The Sapiens had started a fire in the middle of their killing field, and when I analyzed what they were doing, I almost threw up. They were dismembering *and eating* the bodies of the fallen Neanders.

I had to turn away and control my breathing. Then I saw Malaga working his way up the rock pile and I stepped down to stop him.

"No. Stay there. Don't look."

He knew that something was wrong and pushed his way past me.

I didn't move but just waited, watching several others looking up at me from the cave's floor below.

Then the wailing started. I turned to see Malaga kneeled on the mat, sobbing and hitting his fist against a flat rock. Blood soon covered the rock as he kept striking it.

He finally stopped and collapsed to the mat, whimpering and weeping.

These were his people. And this was a clear sign.

The Sapiens would stop at nothing to get to us.

33

I thought I couldn't be further surprised until I got the word from Wren: a sole Sapien was walking toward the cave. Alone and waving a handful of white feathers.

I clambered up the mound to the lookout spot to see.

It was now close to sundown and the Rock cast long shadows over the eastern plain. I saw the Sapien group clustered around their fire and then I saw the man.

He had stopped in the deepening shadows about 100 yards from the cave. He had both of his arms raised above his shoulders and he was speaking directly to us. I couldn't understand the words but I guessed at what he was saying.

He wanted to meet with one of us. He wanted a powwow with a leader, as he surely was.

"*Nuh gook,*" said Wren, who had joined me at the top of the rock pile. He didn't want me to go.

Brassy then appeared on my other side. "*Minya nuh,*" came her words, just as intent and negative as Wren's.

They both knew that I was the one who would have to go meet this Sapien. And they both wanted me not to. So I did the only thing that made sense to me.

I stood up.

I would meet the man. I had to give it a chance. Maybe I could make a deal. Maybe I could reach a compromise with this fellow member of *H. sapiens*. Maybe I could avoid more bloodshed. I had to try.

After checking to make sure I had my quartz blade firmly tied around my waist, I started down the outside of the mounded barrier to meet the enemy under an unspoken sign of truce.

I had no way to know if that's what the white feathers meant to the Sapiens, but I was willing to take the chance.

After I reached the sand and scree of the plain, I walked with a slow, steady pace toward the man. I saw him do the same.

When we were about three yards apart we both stopped and stared at each other. We were studying. Analyzing. Evaluating the other's strengths and weaknesses.

The man certainly looked like a leader. He had a full beard and long, black hair in braids, with multiple eagle feathers protruding out the back. Over his dark skin he wore a thick cape of stitched hide pieces, and from a black necklace hung at least six, curved, bear claws.

A final touch was three stripes of dark red, painted horizontally across his forehead. I quickly realized that those stripes were painted in blood.

The man and I were about the same size. I may have been slightly taller, but he made up for it in muscle mass. And he was younger, although I had found that judging ages was difficult in a time of hard struggle against predators, enemies, and the elements.

He lifted the hand with the white feathers—stork, I guessed—and started to speak in a deep baritone. This was a *Homo sapiens* voice, immediately distinguishable from that of the Neanderthals.

After a few minutes of undecipherable speech and some innovative body signing, my takeaway conclusion was that the man was offering us his terms of surrender. *Our* surrender.

The essence of his proposal boiled down to the overused *trust me, no harm will come to you if you give in to us now.*

Despite the deadly seriousness of the situation, I had to keep myself from laughing out loud. Instead, I just smiled as ambiguously as I could.

I had seen far too many movies and read too many books to believe that this murderous thug was sincere about what he was saying. He didn't know that *don't worry, no harm will come to you* was a cliché in my world.

I didn't believe a word of it and decided to press the

point. I needed to show strength at this moment. Even if I didn't feel it, I had to demonstrate it.

I narrowed my eyes and jabbed a pointed finger at him. As I did this, I opened my mouth and let the words escape in a low pitch that I saturated with menace, intimidation, and self-assurance. I was acting.

"There will be no surrender except from you, you piece of shit."

To add to the effect, I spat on the ground in his direction.

After I saw his eyes widen and his mouth fall open in disbelief, I turned my back to the man and walked away with all the confidence I could summon.

◆ ◆

The only explanation I had for making it back to the cave alive was that I must have stunned the Sapien leader into inaction or paralyzation.

He had probably never met a light-skinned man like me before. Someone who was clearly not a Neanderthal but not exactly like him either. And someone who had stood his ground and challenged him in a very personal way.

I was an alien being to this man. Potential predator? Or prey?

All I know is, my lips and legs were trembling on the way back as I started to see the first stars appear above the Rock. I kept waiting for a blow to the head or an atlatl spear to the back. But nothing happened.

After climbing over the cave's barrier mound, I was greeted by the entire group of Neanders who were trying to make sense of what they had just witnessed.

I was either a courageous leader who deserved a round of their unique style of chest-thumping applause, or I was some kind of magical spirit who could never be understood.

The courageous-leader sentiment won out, and I was soon engulfed by these people who were expressing their appreciation by both slapping me on the back and chest, and singing an impromptu song complete with chants and new birdlike vocalizations.

I let the victory party go on for about five minutes before I raised my arms and asked for quiet.

I jumped on top of a nearby boulder and stood motionless until the crowd noise stopped and all eyes were on me.

"My friends," I started. "My mooka."

"Mooka!" several in the crowd shouted, and that was followed by another round of chest applause. I was one of them.

I waved them down, asking again for silence.

"We are in serious danger."

I motioned to the cave entrance and acted out with clubbing and spearing motions what was waiting for us, all the while making generous references to the *Nuh Minya*. The bad Sapiens.

Everyone grew serious as I'm sure their minds played

back the images they had just seen or the stories they'd been told about the violence that came with these new people from the north.

I watched as their expressions cycled through the emotions of happiness to fear and finally to a hardened determination. They seemed on the edge of motivation to stop these invaders. Ready to do what was needed.

They only required someone to guide them. To tell them what to do.

Just when I felt the crowd energy shift from cautious uncertainty to willing initiative, Rabbit suddenly appeared below me. He was holding up my journal with his small arms. He wanted me to take it.

As I started to bend down, I noticed that the entire crowd went silent, in a reverential sort of way. Like they were witnessing a religious act.

I realized for the first time that the journal had become a type of sacred artifact for them. A symbol of spiritual power. A source of the magic they thought I controlled.

In a way, they weren't far off. I could imagine and do things they could never comprehend.

It wasn't magic to me, of course.

Sometimes it was just basic physics like when I demonstrated how a spear thrower worked. Or how I was able to recall my school-age attempts at drawing to render the world in pen-and-ink in a semi-realistic way on my journal pages. Simple things to me but bordering on sorcery or wizardry to them.

So I took advantage of the moment to thank Rabbit and then raise the journal high in one hand.

As I held it above the crowd of Neanders who surrounded me with focused attention, I saw in my mind the image of a TV evangelist holding up his Bible and urging his enthusiastic audience to *Praise the Lord* or donate to the cause or whatever TV evangelists were famous for.

And I started a soft chant that quickly passed from my lips to the lips of others.

"Minya Nuh, Mooka Gook." Sapiens bad, Neanders good.

It was simplistic. It was crude. But it worked.

I soon had the entire crowd of two dozen Neanderthals chanting in unison with voices that echoed off the cave walls and with eyes that gleamed with strength and intensity.

We were of one mind.

And we were going to war.

34

After sealing the gap at the top of the entrance barrier in the morning, I had to make sure we wouldn't all suffocate from smoke inhalation.

Ironically, Meredith's Cave had been completely blocked by sand and debris when it was first discovered and excavated early in the twentieth century. But the cave might have been wide open for thousands of years before then. So this was probably one of the few times in prehistory that the cave mouth was sealed.

While there was always a certain amount of stuffy smokiness in the cave from the fire that burned continuously, there were plenty of ways for the cave's air to refresh itself. Besides the opening and the two exit routes that snaked and let out under the Rock, several cracks in the ceiling ultimately became crevices that opened up to the outside.

All of these fissures and passages together created a circulation pattern—however slight—to keep the interior air of the cave flowing and breathable.

But I needed to test my belief when there was a blocked entrance. If I was wrong, we would be too dead from carbon monoxide poisoning to realize my mistake.

I lit a small stick from the fire and let it burn while I walked out to the cave's pinch point with a lighted torch in my other hand. With the cave mouth closed, only the dimmest light from the fire reached this narrow spot.

Leaning the burning torch against the wall, I blew out the stick's flame and watched the rising smoke. As soon as the curving vapor trail reached a point just above my head it started to angle back toward the cave's interior. It picked up speed and finally dissipated as it moved horizontally.

The airflow was there.

The next task was to finalize the offensive positions and defensive traps we had already started.

With Wren and Malaga at my side, I checked the overlook positions for the shat and spear throwers.

These were ledges and indentations in the walls that were above head height. They provided good vantage points for launching projectiles down on the enemy. Most had branches, logs, or piled rocks in front to provide both concealment and some protection. Our best throwers would be positioned there.

A special deadfall trap was set up above the narrow passageway that led to the art gallery chamber. A large piece of the wall had pulled away and was leaning precariously over the passage, barely held in place only by its weight and angle.

This had been a hazardous situation for as long as I had been in the cave. And now it would be used to our advantage.

But the main trap was the spiked pitfall. It was a circular hole that stretched across most of the space between the two pinch points that were located about 25 yards inside the cave opening. Two narrow edges allowed people to move safely around the pit.

Carefully covered with a thin layer of branches and debris from the surrounding floor, the trap's main feature was the multiple, sharpened spears that were planted in the hole's bottom pointing up. Anyone who fell through the disguised covering and into the pit would either be impaled on the spears or immobilized and clubbed by those from above.

Everyone else with a weapon—whether a spear, blade, or even just a rock—would be positioned at strategic locations around the cave, ready to stab or strike the enemy.

With the fire doused, the cave would hopefully be inky black, and I was counting on the excellent night vision of the Neanders to confuse and overwhelm the Sapiens until the battle was won.

Because of the extreme dangers involved with the different traps, and also for their general safety, all the children had already been hidden away in the burial chamber. If it came to it, they could escape out the passageway that led to the back of the Rock.

There had been arguments about whether the women of childbearing age should be kept away from the fighting, but Brassy and two of her friends made it clear that they could fight as well as any man, and that had ended the debate.

With the day's preparations done, I walked again with a torch to the pinch point and crouched down on the outside edge of the spiked pit to evaluate its camouflaged covering.

Would it fool the Sapiens? Could it kill or maim at least a couple of them before the ones following discovered it? I certainly hoped so. It was a gruesome trap, but this confrontation had now turned into a binary choice. Either the Sapiens would kill us, or we'd kill them. It was as simple as that.

All at once, I heard voices coming from outside the cave. Deep voices.

I stepped clear of the pit, shouted the command, and waved the torch over my head. I watched the central fire being extinguished and saw people running to their places. I smothered the torch with a piece of reed matting.

I turned and stood still, facing the dark rock pile that blocked the entrance. And I waited.

I focused on my breathing and the smell of pine resin that had burned off the torch. All my senses were alive. I felt like a coiled spring ready to be released.

Then I heard it. A clattering high above me.

I looked up to see a shaft of light burst out of the top of the barrier mound. It grew in size with more sounds of rocks falling. The Sapiens were opening the blockade.

They would soon be in the cave with us.

◆ ◆

I took my position crouching between the feather piles along the north wall. Being farthest out in the cave, my job was to watch the spiked pitfall and gauge the overall strength and numbers of the Sapiens.

Hidden behind a protrusion on the opposite wall was Hand, who stood ready with his favorite bashing club. He had never used it on a man before. Only animals. I hoped he wouldn't lose his nerve.

With the hole in the barrier casting a feeble light over the outermost part of the cave, I could just make out the approaching Sapiens, who were cautiously and silently moving forward. They had no torches and were probably surprised by how dark the cave was. They moved slowly and warily.

I counted eight of them, which meant two more were being held back, including the leader I'd confronted earlier. That was troubling.

Three were in front as scouts, and as they came near the pit I held my breath. In one hand was my blade and in the other a thrusting spear I'd been practicing with.

Please work, I silently mouthed.

I watched while the three men, stooped and close together, stepped slowly forward, scanning left to right, their long braids swinging back and forth.

Then two of them crashed through the pit's cover and immediately cried out in pain. The third man fell back and scrambled away as fast as he could.

"Now!" I shouted to Hand as I sprang forward and rushed to look down into the dark pit.

One of the Sapiens was impaled and still. He was as good as dead.

The other was gored but very much alive. He had bloody spear tips showing through his side and a thigh, and he was writhing like a fish trying to free itself. As soon as he saw me and Hand, he reached up with a free arm and shouted words that I took to mean *help me!*

But helping was the last thing on my mind.

I looked up to see the rest of the Sapiens approaching the pit. I glanced at Hand and nodded down at the man below us.

"Kill him!" I said, making a sharp downward motion with my blade hand. "Use the club."

Hand didn't move. He held the club high but was frozen in place.

This is what I'd feared.

The Neanders were reluctant to use unneeded

violence. Especially violence against other people, no matter that these people had no qualms about using it against *them*.

As someone for whom peace was a goal, I understood the resistance to act violently or heartlessly. However, this was not the time for vacillation or hesitancy. This was do-or-die time. Swift action was required.

Without further thought, I lifted my spear and rammed it down into the man's chest. Hand gasped while the man sputtered and gurgled his last breath.

There was an immediate outcry from the remaining Sapiens who rushed toward us.

I grabbed Hand's arm, spun, and started sprinting away from the pit. Spears, both long and short, whizzed by us as we entered the gloom of the cave's interior.

The battle was on.

35

Hand and I split up before we reached the fire, which still steamed and put out a faint orange glow at its base. Hand went left and I went right to get to one of the ledges.

Because it was so dark, I had to use my hands and feel my way to the north wall and awkwardly climb up to the overlook position.

I immediately bumped into Malaga, who had to grab and hold me with his bandaged hand so I didn't fall off the ledge.

"Minya puk?" he asked.

"Yes, they're coming. Get ready."

I didn't have to worry about any doubts or hesitancy with Malaga. After what he'd been through and witnessed with the Sapiens, I was counting on his desire for revenge to motivate him.

There were several others on the ledge too, but it was hard to see them in the dim light. Only a hint of illumination came from the dying fire and the barrier opening, so I was almost blind. But I knew the Neanders weren't.

"Minya puk," I heard Malaga whisper to both sides and then I heard the sound of shats being handled and spears being nocked to their atlatls.

I strained to see the Sapiens and thought I saw a glimpse of them when I felt Malaga rise up and then heard the whistling sound of his shat slicing through the air. At the same time, I heard more whooshing and whirring as others launched their spear darts.

Almost immediately I heard the Sapiens cry out in pain. The weapons had found their marks.

There was shouting and scuffling below. Then came voices of anger mixed with the sound of dragging.

As the noise diminished I realized that the Sapiens were retreating. They were taking their injured back out of the cave.

We'd chased them away.

For now.

But I knew the Sapiens weren't giving up.

◆ ◆

A chorus of advancing shrieks and howls told us they were back. And with torches to light up the cave.

I counted the full eight running past the feather piles and then the log ring. They must have picked up the other two, including the bearded leader, and prepared themselves for a final assault.

I had moved to the leaning deadfall rock over the passageway that led to the art chamber. Crouching there with Shorty, I watched in alarm as the Sapiens struck down any Neander who tried to stop them.

The attackers had worked themselves into a frenzy and were clubbing, spearing, and stabbing everyone in their way. I saw the Wrestler and several others fall.

The Sapiens were suddenly close.

"Now!" I shouted, pushing against the large rock.

The stone barely budged until Shorty added his remarkable strength to mine and started it moving.

It swayed for a moment then collapsed with a roar and a plume of dust onto the cave floor.

The rock had crushed two of the Sapiens beneath it, and I noticed that one of the torches was now extinguished and the light level in this part of the cave had dropped. I quickly scanned for the other torches and saw only three more.

But I had no time to think about this. The remaining Sapiens seemed more motivated and were attacking anything that moved.

They were winning the battle, overcoming whatever resistance the Neanders—now fighting for their lives—were putting up.

I watched as Malaga valiantly fought off two Sapiens

who had cornered him. But as strong and courageous as he was, he finally succumbed to their clubbing and stabbing.

The situation looked dire. And now I was worried.

Worried that I had let them down. That I hadn't planned enough, or, even worse, that I didn't know what I was doing. I wasn't a soldier, much less a general, and I was losing faith in my ability to protect these people. Was I helping them or doing the opposite?

Then I spotted her.

Brassy was trapped against the far wall of the sleeping chamber with Rabbit. Somehow he had left the children's hiding place and rejoined his mother.

Brassy clutched a long spear and was using it to keep one of the Sapiens away. It was their leader!

He held a torch and was laughing, playing with her by waving the torch and trying to knock the spear from her hands.

I saw Rabbit crouching against the wall, repeatedly hitting his temples with his open hands. He was trying to calm himself and block out the horror around him. The hyena cub was curled in a ball at his feet.

Brassy's eyes turned and fastened on mine. I saw the fear, but I saw something else. A resolute look that reminded me of Carolyn. A determined Carolyn who told me to never give up, no matter how hopeless the situation.

Then I saw the reflection of the man's torch in Brassy's big eyes. *Of course!* The torches.

I leaped from my spot and hit the ground running. I knew what I had to do.

◆ ◆

I reached the Sapien leader just as he was able to wrench Brassy's spear from her with his left hand. His right still held the blazing torch, and that was my focus.

I grabbed the torch at the same time I kicked his legs out from under him.

The man yelled and hit the ground hard, his hair braids bouncing and twisting. He struggled to regain his footing and tried to wield the spear against me, but it was too late.

Using the torch like a club I swung it with all my strength, and it connected with his head. *Thwack!*

The leader was momentarily dazed, but he quickly jumped to his feet and started counterattacking with the spear, jabbing and thrusting.

I was backing up, evading each spear jab when Brassy suddenly jumped on the man's back and started hitting him with a rock. With this distraction, I made my move.

I ran at the man and drove the burning torch hard into his stomach. He bent over and roared with anger.

With Brassy still on his back, I kept pushing the torch against the leader until he finally tripped and fell backward.

He landed right on top of Brassy and she screamed

with pain. But she managed to wriggle out from under the man at the same time I kneeled on top of him.

I still held the flaming torch, and I pushed it harder and deeper into the man. His mouth opened wide and I thought I saw smoke coming out of it.

The fiery end of the torch had burned through his hide covering and was disappearing into his gut. I could see the flesh blistering and hear it sizzling as the fire was gradually put out inside the man's body. The smell of roasted flesh was strong.

As soon as his movements stopped, I stood up over the Sapien leader. In the middle of his body was a singed hole that smoked and hissed. There was hardly any blood because I had both eviscerated and cauterized him at the same time.

I looked up and saw Wren battling nearby with a Sapien holding another torch. Wren must have seen what I had done because he deftly knocked the man's torch away, and I watched as a Neander woman immediately snuffed it out with a handful of matting.

Then I watched Wren attack the man with renewed effort.

One torch left and the cave was sinking into darkness.

This was our chance.

36

"Are you gook?" I asked Brassy, who was cradling her left arm.

"Gook," she said while I gently went over the arm feeling for breaks. There were none. In all likelihood, just a sprain.

Rabbit and the cub had joined us, and I put my arms around all of them and squeezed. I felt tears welling up. We were safe. But for how long?

I lifted my head from our hug and spotted the final torch in the hand of a Sapien near the fire pit. He held a heavy club with his other arm, and he was fighting against three Neanders who surrounded him.

Surprisingly, the Sapien was able to hold off the shorter Neanders. They seemed frightened of this taller man who showed no fear and bellowed with determined aggression.

But the Neanders also moved more slowly and looked exhausted. Just like I had noticed earlier, they were built for shorter bursts of activity rather than endurance. They faded with extended effort.

I was drained, too. It felt like an entire day had dragged by since the Sapiens first pushed through the barrier. I hadn't eaten anything nor had a drop to drink. I was getting the shakes, not sure if from lack of nourishment or from all the tension and conflict.

But something had to be done. We had to douse that final torch.

I was about to start moving toward the fire pit when I heard the familiar noise.

It started with a torrent of high-pitched squeaks that was soon followed by the sound of a million wings fluttering.

The bats!

This was the end-of-day ritual where a horde of the creatures that dwelled high up in the arched vault of Meredith's Cave flew out to feed on insects after sundown.

I stopped where I was and watched the dark mass fly by. It created a strong current of air that washed down on us and kicked up a dust cloud on the ground.

The fighting Sapien froze and then dropped low to avoid being hit by the wave.

Probably more used to open spaces, he seemed confused and afraid of the black shadow that whooshed over his head toward the narrow opening at the mouth of the cave.

And in the process, he let his torch fall.

I jumped to my feet and sprinted toward him with every ounce of energy I still had.

I reached the torch at the same time the man regained his composure—and purpose. We both lunged at each other and came down together on top of the flame.

We grappled and rolled on the ground, using our fists to pummel and pound. I got off some good punches but so did he. We were closely matched. And tiring at the same time.

As soon as I noticed that the torch was out and the cave had become very dark, I pushed myself away from the fight. I could barely see my opponent, which meant he couldn't see me.

But the Neanderthals could see.

◆ ◆

By my estimate, there were only four attackers left. And fewer than ten of us able to fight. But the advantage had shifted. The Sapiens would be almost blind, as I was, in this dark and dim cave. The Neanders, however, would have their improved sight.

I pictured it like they were wearing military night-vision goggles, but built into their heads. To be sure, the advantage was slight, but now was the time to make the most of it.

The Sapiens were stumbling around and trying to get oriented in the pitch-dark cave—I could hear them calling to each other and cursing when they ran into or tripped over something.

I felt my way back to Brassy. I had to get the next idea across to her. And quickly. My language classes had covered the five basic senses, and I hoped Brassy had been paying attention.

I grabbed her good hand and put it over my eyes at the same time I said, "Tum kuk no see. Minya no see."

She was just a dark shape, but I could imagine her mind trying to make sense of what I was saying.

"Minya no see?" she said.

I heard a loud cry and a curse nearby from one of the Sapiens. I felt her react so I knew she heard it, too.

"Minya no see," I repeated. "But Mooka see."

She grabbed my hand firmly in hers and placed it over her face. "Minya no see. Mooka see."

I touched her shoulder with my other hand and squeezed. "Gook."

She understood. But would the others?

Then, as if intuiting my question, she started singing. It was like nothing I'd heard before. It was a warbling whistle but with an urgency to it. Like the warning call of an animal in trouble.

I was worried the sound would attract the Sapiens, but almost immediately I heard other Neanders singing back. The sounds were now coming from every direction and echoing off the cave walls. The Sapiens would be completely confused.

And before I knew it, the Neanders were gathering around us.

We were still in the sleeping chamber at the very back of the cave, and I could only see their dark outlines and hear their breathing and smell their sweat. It looked like all the adult survivors had come, including Wren. Maybe eight to ten.

Brassy spoke rapidly to the group. She reached over to me at one point and I heard grunting all around. These were grunts of nervous affirmation.

As quickly as they had come, the group dispersed. And within minutes of their leaving I heard the first shriek of pain from an unlucky Sapien somewhere in the cave.

And then more.

37

Two days of burials and mourning had consumed us.

We'd won the battle and now it was time to deal with the two remaining Sapien survivors. Tied up outside the cave entrance, they were still covered in dried blood and wincing from their broken bones.

There had been a long debate around the relit fire the night before. I urged that the two be eliminated. They were severely injured anyway and would probably welcome a swift end.

But my main point was to keep them from regrouping and coming back with a larger force. The Neanders had used their night vision advantage to overcome their fears and indecision and prevail over the Sapiens. But one battle doesn't win the war, and I knew what history had in store for the Neanderthals.

Unless I had now changed that history.

Instead of events from this point flowing toward ultimate *Homo sapiens* dominance of the world, maybe I was adding a curve to the timeline. A turn or a twist that rippled downstream toward a different future.

But I lost the prisoner debate, and we now released and pushed the two Sapiens down the slope with our spear points and our verbal threats. They didn't dare look back or argue and were soon limping out of sight on a path northward.

I gave them a 50 percent chance of surviving. And if they did, they would tell the story of fighting a strong group of Neanderthals with a mysteriously magical white man leading them into battle.

Maybe that would give them pause. Maybe they would leave Meredith's Cave alone. Or maybe not.

The celebration had already started at the main fire by the time I arrived.

I had delayed my return, waiting for the Sapiens to disappear, but even more, spending time alone looking out toward the line of cairns in the distance. And thinking about Carolyn. And Victoria. And my boss. And all the rest of my world in 2019. If that world even existed as I remembered it.

I was conflicted with a mix of emotions.

There was the anticipation of going back. I could share my knowledge of what Neanderthals were really like. I would be famous. And finally make some real money.

Plus the excitement of changing history. Of helping to create a different world.

Offsetting this was the hollow feeling of sorrow and despair in never having a life with Carolyn and our baby. The joy of that family's future was gone. Ripped from me in a moment of violence.

And finally, there was the unsettledness of being both in the present and the past. In a type of limbo. Without order or stability. The kind of anxious state that would have easily triggered my OCD behaviors before. Although I felt myself moving beyond those old patterns now.

When I reached the fire I was greeted by the entire band dancing in a circle and chanting. I stood to the side and watched for a while.

The grieving from the Sapien battle had ended and the Neanders seemed absolutely carefree. Shorty was dancing with both his wives who were not arguing but smiling. Wren, nursing two injuries, gamely shuffled along while holding his daughter Tepela on his shoulders. Hand danced and spun with his wife.

Then I located Brassy. She was dancing backward holding Rabitt's hands. And the hyena cub was running and jumping up alongside them. They were turning circles and laughing.

I envied them their untroubled attitude. I still had doubts and concerns. Many.

Brassy spotted me and waved me in with that enigmatic smile. I slapped my chest two times to break my mood and walked to join them in the dance circle. My worries could take a break.

◆ ◆

The next day, I found Brassy and Rabbit at the flat-topped boulder down the slope from the cave entrance. A thin cloud cover had rolled in during the night, diffusing the midday sun and casting soft shadows. It was now February, the windiest month, and a chilly breeze had brought out the heavier hide coverings we all wore.

This was the spot where I had first introduced Rabbit and the group to the enchantment of journal writing. And Rabbit had taken to it like a natural scribbler.

The boy was beginning to understand the concept of letters, although he preferred drawing. He still liked his straight-line designs, but he was experimenting with sketching and drawing from nature. Trees, flowers, animals ... whatever was around him.

I hung back to study the domestic scene in front of me. It looked almost like a bucolic 17th-century tableau painted by a Dutch or Italian master, only without the crops and cows.

Rabbit sat cross-legged on the rock engrossed in the journal, trying to render the face of his friend Tepela. But she kept making faces at him and playing with the two cackling hyena cubs. Another cub had recently been rescued and brought into the group. This wasn't yet the dog-type domestication program I was hoping for, but it was moving in that direction.

Brassy kneeled on the ground nearby with Shorty's wife Chubby, each chewing a strip of deerskin. Even though they were busy, they still made time to gossip and laugh together.

Shorty and Wren were lying on their backs, heads together, napping.

I envied this family setting. I'd never had a real family to belong to. Always the outsider, the loner.

Until Carolyn and the baby, now both a memory.

I crouched down next to the thorn bush that partially concealed me. What was I doing? Why was I rushing to get back to my other world? Here was a group that accepted me. Warmly welcomed me. Even revered me.

As strange as the situation was, I had found an actual home here at Meredith's Cave. Something—somewhere—to be a part of.

Especially when I considered my unique circumstances and my influence on not just this group of people and their survival, but—and I snorted at the audacity of it—on the future of humanity. I was literally changing the future with every action I took in 40 kya.

Exactly how, I wasn't sure, but why couldn't I distort the arc of history even more to incorporate the best parts of what I saw in my Neanders? A gentleness. Empathy and caring. An aversion to violence.

Why not?

I stood and walked to join the group.

The hyena cubs immediately flew to me, squirming and yipping. Tepela called out my name, and Brassy and Chubby both looked up and waved.

I sat down on the boulder next to Rabbit and peeked over his shoulder. His drawing of Tepela was no worse than anything I would have done at his age. Honestly, he was a better artist.

I patted him on the head.

"Gook. Good job."

Tepela came up and held out her right hand. She was offering me a small stone.

"*Stuk,*" she said in her high voice.

I took the stone and examined it. White, perfectly round, and worn smooth. Probably from the distant shore.

"Gook stuk," I said, realizing the stone was roughly the size of the totem ring I still wore around my neck. I reached up to touch it.

I sensed movement and looked up to see Chubby, Wren, and Shorty all standing and beckoning to Rabbit and Tepela. I didn't understand all the words but the meaning quickly became clear: they were leaving me alone with Brassy.

For a brief moment, I felt as if I were watching a romantic comedy. I shook my head and smiled. I knew what they were doing, and I found myself not objecting.

Brassy walked over and sat next to me on the flat stone. The clouds had vanished and the rock was warm under the afternoon sun.

We both watched wordlessly while the group disappeared into the cave.

I turned to look at Brassy at the same time I moved my knee to touch hers.

She looked down, then pressed her knee to mine before looking back up. Her electric blue eyes shone against her tanned skin and auburn hair, and her lips turned up into a smile. Less enigmatic this time.

"Gook?" she said in a whisper.

I grabbed the thong around my neck and pulled it over my head.

"Gook," I said, untying the knot and releasing the diamond ring.

I reached for her left hand and brought it close.

Taking hold of her ring finger, I tried to slip the ring on but it didn't fit. I moved to the little finger and the ring slid on perfectly.

Brassy looked down in surprise, then held her hand up to me, displaying the ring with obvious pride.

"Wife?"

"Wife," I said with conviction as I pulled her close.

I was staying.

38

Dr. Victoria Busher pulled on her special exam gloves and carefully opened the journal again. It had become her Sunday habit with the museum closed. And she needed to finalize her keynote speech for the Neanderthal conference in Germany the following week.

Rain slashed the front windows while she studied the final pages of the journal. Exactly one year had passed since she'd arrived back from 40 kya.

So much had happened in a year.

She'd reached the level of science fame she had aimed for after discovering Tom's journal.

He had placed it inside a piece of crude, fired-clay pottery. A thin box packed with acidic moss, which turned the enclosure into a miniature version of a pickling bog.

The cover was damaged and the paper yellowed, but the ink was still readable. The oldest journal in the world.

It was buried in the nearby cave close to where she and Tom had last sat and talked before her coming back to the present. No one had thought to excavate there, but she had guessed that Tom would have picked a secure place she was familiar with, and that would eventually be covered under tons of sand and debris and lost to the world for thousands of years.

Soon after returning, she'd instructed the dig team to go down deeper at the distinctive vertical crack by the entrance.

The combination of the artifacts and notes she'd brought back plus Tom's exquisitely detailed journal and other datable deposits had changed not only her life—on top of her tenure she was now the Visiting Director of the Gibraltar Natural History Museum—but the way the world thought about Homo neanderthalensis.

How human and modern they really were. And how much their DNA had influenced the evolution of Homo sapiens.

But what she'd kept to herself was how right Tom had been. About the changes. How their travel to the past had affected the present. At least, this version of the present.

The wars in the Middle East. Terrorism. Political partisanship. They had all happened but there were significant differences now. Getting along was more important than she remembered. So was community and kindness.

The world—this rendition of it—was truly a gentler place than before her journey through time. The violence that had marked so much of the other life had dissipated.

The butterfly had taken wing.

Plus, the Neanderthals had gone extinct much later. Instead of 30–40,000 years ago, the endpoint was now accepted to be 12 kya, or on the border of the Pleistocene and Holocene time periods.

The entire archaeological record had been altered with more finds in more locations. She couldn't help but think that Tom—and maybe she—had something to do with that.

And her guesses about why she never saw him again were proven right by the journal.

She turned to the last pages and reread the section aloud to herself.

> IT'S GETTING HARDER FOR BRASSY TO MOVE AROUND. HER BELLY IS HUGE. EVERYONE IS EXCITED ABOUT THE COMING BABY. RABBIT'S HOPING FOR A BROTHER TO PLAY WITH AND THE HYENA PACK HAS NOW EXPANDED TO FOUR. WREN IS GLAD TO SEE HIS SISTER HAPPY. BUT NO ONE IS MORE THRILLED

THAN ME. I'LL FINALLY HAVE MY
FAMILY. AND IF IT'S A GIRL WHO
CAN PASS ON HER MITOCHONDRIAL DNA,
THEN THERE'S HOPE FOR THE FUTURE
OF BOTH OUR SPECIES.

So Tom's temporary pause in returning to their present had finally morphed into the permanent one that he'd hinted at.

Victoria closed the journal and walked to the spotlighted display case, lifting the lid and placing the journal back in its prominent position on the slanted backboard.

She closed and locked the lid and stepped back to admire the collection. She had agreed to a museum exhibit in the end. More visitors would see it this way.

Next to the journal was the skeletal hand with the ring. Brassy's hand, with Carolyn's ring. Tom's original photo of its discovery in the cave was propped up next to it. She was sure he was the one who'd put the ring on Brassy's finger in 40 kya.

She chuckled as she imagined Tom on his knees proposing to his Neanderthal girlfriend, with her peculiar voice, tangled hair, and rough manner. Victoria couldn't help but feel a little jealous of her, but the signs had been there all along.

In the end, she wasn't really surprised. Tom had had a difficult life. And if he was happy, then she would be happy for him.

Victoria heard the door open and turned to see her assistant, Lucía, shaking the rain off her umbrella. She was Santiago's sister and a good worker. She joined her at the display case.

"It's true he could have come back with you but stayed?" Lucía asked with her good English, Llanito accented.

Victoria regarded the piece of rawhide shoelace and the pierced shell that were displayed on the other side of the journal. Her time-travel totems.

"It's true. And he did us all a favor."

"A favor?"

She studied Lucía for a moment, noting her dark olive skin and watching her fidget, knowing she couldn't light one of her ever-present cigarettes in the museum. Both were traits she could have inherited from her Neanderthal ancestors.

"He changed our world."

"Really? How?"

Victoria sighed. "It's a long story.

She started to walk away but felt Lucía touch her arm.

"Do you think about him sometimes?"

She paused. "I do. And I know he was content in the end."

Lucía looked puzzled.

"Content? Living in such a primitive time?"

Victoria smiled, mostly for herself.

"He found what he wanted."

Afterword

At the end of my last novel (*New York 1609*), I spent several pages addressing both the veracity of the book's historical presentations, and also what had happened in the intervening 400 years after my story closed.

But that novel is what I like to call "pure historical fiction." That is, the reader is transported in time and place to a distant past (officially, per novel-writing conventions, at least 50 years before the present). And they stay planted there as the story unfolds.

In this case, with *Neander*, not only do I include both the past and the present (via the useful tool of time travel), but there is a big difference when one goes way back into the past to, say, 40,000 years ago.

For one thing, there are no written records or documents to guide the author in understanding the world of the Neanderthals and other archaic or developing humans in that time frame. Clues to our origins in prehistory mainly lie buried under the ground in the form of artifacts, other situational evidence, or, if we're lucky, skeletal remains that are discovered, excavated, and analyzed.

And a new tool for paleoanthropological study was announced in 2010: the complete sequencing of the Neanderthal genome by preeminent geneticist Svante Pääbo and his team at the Max Planck Institute for Evolutionary Anthropology.

This ancient DNA has given us even more insights into the prehistoric lives of our cousins on the hominid family tree.

But there are still plenty of unanswered questions.

And I've had to adapt my guiding principle in writing fiction about the past, which I borrow from author Ken Follett: that the events depicted either *did* happen, or they *could have* happened.

Now, what I can do is to say that while many of the events in this book could have taken place as described, there are certain elements—like traveling through time—that I will leave to the realm of the imagination.

In the meantime, the debates about what caused the demise of the Neanderthals continue. In my research, I've discovered at least a dozen theories that attempt to explain this mystery. Everything from outright genocide to climate change to Neanders being more prone to ear infections.

So, are we closer to understanding why our species—*Homo sapiens*—rules the planet today and not Neanderthals, who, after all, existed for many thousands of years longer than we have?

Possibly.

And new discoveries will surely come. Which means that some of my assumptions may become obsolete as time goes on.

The future holds the key.

And the past.

> — Harald Johnson
> Charlottesville, Virginia
> Fall Equinox, 2019

Acknowledgments

This book project started with my usual walks in the woods around my house and my workout sessions at a local swimming pool.

During these times, I like to let my mind wander and pose untethered *What if . . . ?* questions to myself. Sometimes loopy ones. Like: *What if I write about traveling back in time to the Middle Ages?*

Well, that's already been done—and done well—by others like Mark Twain (*A Connecticut Yankee in King Arthur's Court*) and Michael Crichton (*Timeline*).

What if I went back further in time?

Rome? Done.

Ancient Egypt? Done.

Then, while doing a lazy backstroke and staring at the clouds at the outdoor pool one day in the fall of

2018, I had a thought. One that made me sprint to the pool's edge and jump out to grab a notebook I always kept close at hand.

I had been reading Yuval Harari's nonfiction book *Sapiens: A Brief History of Humankind* every night, so I wrote this: *What about Neanderthals?* They were our closest and latest human relatives. And they had mysteriously disappeared sometime between 30–40,000 years ago. And for a short while, we (*Homo sapiens*) coexisted with them.

What if I wrote about Neanderthals during a time when they interacted with Sapiens?

Now there was a potential story.

Of course, I wasn't the first to think of this. Not by a long shot.

Ever since the discovery of the first skeletal remains of *Homo neanderthalensis* in 1856 in the Neander Valley of Germany, people have been fascinated by this other species (or "race" as some suggest) that most closely resembles our own. And that includes writers of novels.

One early example is J.H. Rosny-Aîné and his *La Guerre du Feu*, published in 1911. You probably know it better for its film adaptation: *Quest for Fire* (1981).

Another story that puts Neanderthals in contact (and conflict) with Early Modern Humans (Sapiens) is the best-selling *The Clan of Cave Bear* series by Jean M. Auel (1980-).

Two other interesting books in this all-in-the-past vein are: William Golding's *The Inheritors* (1955) and

Björn Kurtén's *Dance of the Tiger* (1980).

And the list goes on. And with permutations.

There are novels where living Neanderthals are miraculously discovered in remote locations today. The "Lost World" scenario. John Darnton's *Neanderthal* (1996) and Philip Kerr's *Esau* (1997) are prime examples.

Another category involves Neanderthal "de-extinction," where either Neanderthals have evolved to be our superiors (*Neanderthal Parallax* trilogy, Robert J. Sawyer (2002-2010), or Neanderthals are cloned from ancient DNA in the manner of *Jurassic Park* (*The Neanderthals Are Back*, Gini Graham Scott (2019).

Then there are the "split-time" novels that bounce back and forth between the present day and the ancient past, where something physical or psychological links the two tracks. Examples include: Claire Cameron's *The Last Neanderthal* (2017) and Harper Swan's *The Replacement Chronicles* (2019).

Finally, we have a vast number of scientific articles, research studies, and nonfiction books that look into the key questions: Who were the Neanderthals? How did they differ from us Sapiens? And what finally caused their extinction? (Keep in mind that some believe they never did go extinct but, instead, live within us today.)

A sampling of good books by these scientists and researchers include: *The Third Chimpanzee: The Evolution and Future of the Human Animal* by Jared Diamond

(1992); *The Last Neanderthal: The Rise, Success, and Mysterious Extinction of Our Closest Human Relatives* by Ian Tattersall (1995); *The Humans Who Went Extinct: Why Neanderthals Died Out and We Survived* (2009) and *The Smart Neanderthal: Bird Catching, Cave Art & the Cognitive Revolution* (2019) by Clive Finlayson; *The Invaders: How Humans and Their Dogs Drove Neanderthals to Extinction* by Pat Shipman (2015); *The Neanderthals Rediscovered: How Modern Science Is Rewriting Their Story* by Dimitra Papagianni and Michael A. Morse (2013); the important *Neanderthal Man: In Search of Lost Genomes* by Svante Pääbo (2014); and *The Singing Neanderthals: The Origins of Music, Language, Mind and Body* (2006) by Steven Mithen, which inspired my story's communal chanting.

A word about time travel, another classic subgenre of novel writing.

I decided to create a time-travel bridge in *Neander* that connected the modern with the prehistoric past. A way for a contemporary character to actually visit and interact with characters in the long-ago.

And again, I'm not the first to do this. My favorite exemplars are: Jack Finney's classic *Time and Again* (1970), Michael Crichton's *Timeline* (1999), Stephen King's brilliant *11/22/63* (2011), and Blake Crouch's multiverse approach in *Dark Matter* (2016).

Sometimes there's a time machine or device involved, other times drugs or self-hypnosis. And sometimes there's just a strange time portal that can whisk someone away for no apparent reason.

As you can imagine, I have read and studied all the books mentioned above. And many more. And I continue to keep up with the latest discoveries about *Homo neanderthalensis*.

I don't claim to be an expert in any of these areas of research or investigation, but they all helped to inspire and inform me in the creation of the work you hold in your hands, whether analog or digital.

So while I've tried to be faithful to whatever historical record is known about our hominid lineage in the Upper Paleolithic era—as well as the unusual ability to travel through time—I've also taken the fiction writer's prerogative of filling in the gaps with my creative powers. Which means that any historical, anthropological, or theoretical errors are entirely my own.

◆ ◆

More personally, I want to thank the individuals who had a direct hand in helping me create this book.

Jennifer Quinlan of Historical Editorial provided her professional and all-important editing skills to the original manuscript drafts.

I also received important feedback from beta readers Ian Sawyer in Sutton Coldfield, England, and Richard Marks in Los Angeles.

Additional input (and support) came from my enthusiastic Founding Fans "street team," and all the followers of my website and Facebook pages.

Plus, I thank the indie-publishing bloggers and authors I've had the pleasure to interact with in this brave new world of independent publishing. Their advice and friendship are much valued.

And, of course, a great deal of appreciation goes to my current and future readers. Without you, there would be little reason to keep writing.

Finally, my deepest thanks go to my wife and partner, Lynn, who continues to believe in me.

About the Author

Harald Johnson is an author of both fiction and nonfiction, a publisher, and a lifelong swimmer—who actually swam around New York's Manhattan island. His debut novel (*New York 1609*, 2018) was the first-ever to explore the birth of New York City (and Manhattan) from its earliest beginnings. This is his second novel.

Harald loves standing in—or imagining—important places from history and drifting back through the timestream to re-experience them. In the present, he lives with his wife deep in the woods of central Virginia.

Website: http://haraldjohnson.com

Made in the USA
Coppell, TX
06 July 2020